The Sea Family

The Sea Family

Diana Raymond

PIATKUS

Copyright © 1997 by Diana Raymond

First published in Great Britain in 1997 by
Judy Piatkus (Publishers) Ltd of
5 Windmill Street, London W1

The moral right of the author has been asserted

A catalogue record for this book is available from the British Library

ISBN 0–7499–0373–2

Set in 11/12pt Times by
Action Typesetting Ltd, Gloucester
Printed and bound in Great Britain by
Butler & Tanner Ltd, Frome and London

With Loving Memories
of
Ernest Raymond
(who loved Freshwater)
and
Margaret Lucy Lightfoot

Chapter 1
Kate – 1940

The box was black, tin, the paint scratched, the initials I.S.C. faintly discernible. It was not large – Kate had found it quite easy to lift, to take from the storage department of Barker's in Kensington, to a taxi. The taxi driver – like all taxi drivers at this time – had been eager to talk of last night's raid and give details of a near miss in Piccadilly (again, all taxi drivers have had a near miss.) But Kate Lewis, thirty-two, articulate, usually open-handed with taxi drivers, both in cash and conversation, had answered him absently, lighting a cigarette; she had made sure at this time that she wouldn't run out of cigarettes.

''Ave to turn left here, miss. Roped off, something unexploded.'

She saw the notice, familiar now – UXB – and said, 'Yes, sure; you turn left.' Something unexploded? She glanced at the box beside her. You might say that, she thought. You might perhaps say that. I've yet to find out.

She reached home, a flat near Victoria, in the November dusk. Having paid off the taxi driver with an overlarge tip, she climbed the stairs because a recent raid had put the lift out of action. Her living room, small, cluttered, bore the marks of most rooms at this time – dust, curtailed light because of sticking tape on the window, a lingering metallic smell, perhaps the aftermath of explosive. Here she put down the box and sat – cigarette in hand – making no further effort to move. So long as she didn't turn on the light there was no need to draw the black-out curtains, and this she was glad of, not wanting to be enclosed in the room.

1

Not long ago she would have had small time for such a concern, being by nature impatient of unnecessary fuss. But this was a new time.

She glanced again at the box. I.S.C. – Isabel St Clair. Her grandmother, recently dead, at a great age. Not like that other death, not at all like... A narrow crack of pain, like the sliver of light through an opening door, threatened to extend itself, and she moved quickly to the window. In these recent days movement, if not a palliative, had at least been better than staying still.

She could discern the Warden's Post, and the large S above the air raid shelter, swaddled with sandbags. Protection. Possible safety. But there hadn't been safety enough... That's enough of that, she told herself. You have to shut the door. Not really possible, of course. She had learned this, among other things. Having few illusions about herself, Kate was surprised to find that, together with passion, a lively sense of the absurd, and an inability to remain solvent, she had this willingness to learn. For in new territory you had to learn your way about, you were a stranger in this part of the wood. In this dark and sometimes frightening part of the wood.

Abruptly, changing her mind (as she frequently did) she pulled the black-out curtains, enclosing the room, and turned on the light. Light made more of the dust, the crumbs of broken glass. She observed these with detachment, acknowledging the inertia of grief. Dust didn't matter, scattered glass didn't matter. Nothing really mattered.

Except perhaps the box. Strange that the relic of a grandmother should offer a tinge of comfort. Because of the question marks, the things unknown? She lifted the box and put it on the desk below the shrouded window. She did this with some reverence, as if it were a holy thing. Well, perhaps it was holy in a way, as all the past is holy, being lost, no longer subject to time. Grandmother Isabel had died at the end of a long life – how long no one was quite certain, and she herself had perhaps forgotten. A mysterious life, for she spoke little of the past. Yet Kate could recall in her presence a vibration on the air, words unsaid. She never mentioned the box. If questioned, she would say, 'It's nothing. An old woman's secrets. And these are dull. Best forgotten.'

2

Perhaps. But I am not convinced that her secrets are dull, Kate thought. What were the facts about Grandmother Isabel? She had been a widow for many years; her husband, Alexander, had died long ago. Family legend had it that Alexander was a devoted churchman, even, it was said, a kind of saint. In Kate's view, saints were rare, and Grandmother – if she spoke of him at all – only murmured, 'Your Grandfather,' on a lost sigh, and made no reference to sainthood. Yet the name Alexander pulsed with a small drumbeat of mystery: Kate could remember her mother saying, 'Something happened.' When asked what, her mother shook her head. 'None of us knew. Your grandmother wasn't always kind to him. She didn't go to church as he did.' This didn't seem to Kate an extreme of brutality, yet the question remained.

'Something happened.' Kate put a hand idly on the box and it seemed that an electric current that had passed between them – the old woman, so near her end, and her granddaughter – still persisted. Even though such a little while ago Kate had seen her body go silently to the flames and had walked away into the winter's cold, with a small company.

She recalled the unwelcome ceremony, the place of final departure. There had been a stranger there; she had noticed him especially for the company was indeed small, a wartime gathering, herself and her younger cousin, Perdita, in London for the funeral and lodging with Kate. The stranger wore an overcoat with the collar turned up; he looked to be in his sixties, face carved with lines, hair thickly grey. He sat alone in a back pew in the small ungrateful room. As they came out into the winter air, she had glanced at him with curiosity and received an answering look of what might have been sardonic sympathy. She had supposed that he would linger at some point, and that they would have a chance to speak, but when she looked again, he had disappeared. So rapidly that she had the disturbing sense that perhaps she had imagined him, or even that he had been a ghost. She said to Perdita, 'Did you see an elderly man in an overcoat just now?'

Perdita who, though she was younger and more diffident, always picked up what was unspoken, said, 'Yes, he wasn't an apparition; he had a lived-in face and was somehow familiar, though I don't think I've ever seen him before.'

Perdita had two small children and a husband in the RAF (Bomber Command); she was staying 'for the duration' – or as long as she could stand it – with her mother-in-law in Cumberland, to keep the children out of harm's way. She had not yet seen the box, but she would, Kate decided, be as interested in it as she herself was. More perhaps, being younger and remembering Isabel mostly in her old age, when her wits, if not her quiet benignity, had begun to fail. She did just remember that Isabel believed that one could dream ahead, and she didn't consider this absurd. We are, Kate reflected, rather an odd family – though perhaps all families are odd – and ready to believe in mysteries. Sometimes Isabel's mind wandered – but you couldn't always be sure whether the wandering had purpose or not. Sometimes she said she could hear the sea, even when she was far inland. 'The sea tells me things,' she murmured. 'I learn things when I walk by the sea.' In the old people's home where Isabel spent her last years, a nurse would say, 'Yes, dear, of course you do,' moving quickly on, but Kate was not so sure this was nonsense.

For instance, Kate wondered, how much did she know about me? More than I told her, perhaps; there was that look on her face sometimes when I talked to her, a look of secret amusement as if she listened to something other than my voice. You do not, after all, tell your grandmother about your love affairs, your occasional bouts of strong drinking, the extreme difficulties you had – and still have – in remaining solvent. (Though these came not so much from extravagance as a need – in the past – to settle her mother's debts.) You told Isabel the good things – that your last book had been successful – exaggerating a little – both here and in the States. And, if good thing it was, that on the outbreak of war you had, to everyone's surprise, decided to join the ATS.

You told her that joining the services was like going back to school.

'*Lewis!*'

'*Yes, ma'am?*'

'*Simply because you have made some kind of a name for yourself in the bookshops doesn't mean you can do what you like in the Army.*'

'*No, ma'am, I never thought it did. What did I do wrong?*'

4

Yes, just like school. But it was no longer possible to tell her that now, again, just like school, she had run away. Or at least, extended compassionate leave beyond its time.

So that here in the small London room she had the sensation of one who had gone to ground, to some place of hiding. She couldn't, of course, hide for long. ATS Section Commanders who overstayed their leave would be sought out and brought back to HQ. Kate briefly looked aside to the memory of the windy seaside town, the bleak Company HQ, the groups of ill-matched young women, thrown together by the circumstances of war. A winter town, smelling of the sea and prepared against invasion; barbed wire and concrete drums on the beach. Would she return? Large hurdles ahead – large questions, one especially which demanded resolution. She had not yet made up her mind.

I am in limbo, she thought, which is not a good place. Maybe it's where I deserve to be; most likely so. But it has no sure boundaries, no clear maps, and I'm used to maps...

Here came the sound of the siren, the familiar swooping wail, followed almost at once by the drumbeat of anti-aircraft guns. And her cousin, Perdita, was somewhere in the London streets. I'd like her back, Kate thought absently. Safely back. But the word 'safely' brings the memory sharply alive.

No, she had never spoken to her grandmother about Charles.

Not one to do things by halves (Kate was clear about that), she had loved Charles Seddon with total commitment for five years. What, she wondered, would she have said to Isabel? That he had been married, a marriage which had been dead for a long time – or so he always said. (Yes, darling, though I grieve for you to the depths of my heart, I have no illusions.) That, working in the Home Office, he had an official engagement in Coventry. They had, of course, made jokes about being sent to Coventry – not very good jokes, just the kind that lovers make. 'I don't like leaving you in London,' he'd said. And indeed, danger, such as it was, seemed to be centred on the city. She had not allowed for the Luftwaffe's change of plan.

Coventry. When she heard the news of destruction, to begin with, though much afraid, she had not believed the worst. It was Charles' sister, Harriet, who had telephoned her. Harriet had been a confidante, neutral maybe, not unsympathetic. Her voice on the telephone had at once sent a current of dread through Kate's stomach. 'Kate, I'm afraid I've got bad news. I know this is awful for you, but I have to tell you. Charles was killed in the Coventry raid. The hotel he was staying in had a direct hit. They say there've been lots of casualties – the worst raid of the war. Kate dear, I'm very sorry.'

Yes, that brought memory back. The savage moment of loss, the last wave of the hand, the slam of the door. The loved voice was loud in her ears, but she would never hear it again. Never.

'And I'm bloody well not going to cry,' she said aloud. There was a sensation like extreme cramp in her chest, but it needn't resolve itself in tears. And now the anti-aircraft guns were louder and she could hear the drone of enemy aircraft. Danger, perhaps. But now it didn't matter, because nothing mattered. What was there to protect, to save, to cherish?

Perhaps it was time now to open the box.

It had been a long while in the storage vault, and the catch was rusty – even, it seemed, locked – but she wasn't at this stage going to be thwarted by that. She found a screwdriver and steadily, but still with a kind of reverence, prised it open.

At first she was disappointed, for on the top she discovered only simple things – inventories, lists of names and addresses, old Christmas cards – poignant now, but just the litter that accumulates after any life. Then, from this small collection of old paper, she drew out a photograph.

'But I remember this!' she said aloud. It was taken at Freshwater Bay in the Isle of Wight, and there was a rumour that it was the work of Julia Margaret Cameron, but someone (she had forgotten who) disagreed and said the dates weren't right: Julia Margaret Cameron, that formidable female photographer, friend of Tennyson, living at the house called 'Dimbola', had died in 1879, and this must have been taken later. How easily the past slips into ignorance.

The photograph showed the whole family: Alexander and Isabel, sitting with their brood about them. Grandfather Alex had a powerful look of achievement, as if these four children were the result of a deal he'd struck with the Almighty, and out of which Alexander had come best. Isabel had the look she always had of containing secrets which gave her perhaps pleasure, perhaps regret.

The photograph absorbed her, while the sounds of the raid increased. The captured moment all those years ago: Marigold, the eldest child (Kate's mother) had her chin up, showing confidence and the beginning of a smile (she was perhaps nine); Rebecca – perhaps seven – looked solemn (but there is always one child who does); Sylvia looked bewildered, though she was the prettiest. Toby the only boy amongst three sisters, stared out with infant expectation from his mother's arms.

Oh God, Kate thought, looking at that far moment of innocence, if only they knew. She looked at Isabel, so quietly proud of her children. You hoped so much for them, Kate thought, and when the harsh blows fell, you must have desperately grieved. But you never talked about them, you never told the whole story. A young, untroubled face, a figure dressed in the clothes of the late eighteen-hundreds. How much did you know? Kate wondered. How much did you foresee?

This photograph was surely taken in the garden of Rosecroft, the house on the island; the house which was later a haven for Charles and Kate together, so that she had come to love the island place as she believed her grandmother had.

The faces, the young faces. They seemed to say, 'This is how we were before the dark truth came to meet us. This is how we all are at one time, in innocence, in the Garden of Eden, before knowledge, before the exile from Paradise.' Alexander, the magnificent (perhaps saintly) Alexander; Isabel in her secret ambiguous dream, and their children, not knowing what was to come. Across the years, in this time of limbo, Kate thought, they seemed to speak to her.

She searched further in the box.

Below the ordinary, inconsiderable papers – the lists, letters which merely confirmed dates, 'on Tuesday, then', some lost Tuesday – she found a number of black exercise books, their covers shabby, their binding loose. The pages within were frayed also, filled with slanted handwriting which at first looked easy, but then proved difficult to read. Isabel's hand, that much was clear. But one hadn't thought of her writing this privately, pages and pages of it, simply for herself.

While the guns kept their aggressive accompaniment, Kate began to read. At first she turned impatiently through the pages, for every now and again the handwriting defeated her. It seemed also that Isabel began each entry with a remark about the weather – 'a cold blowy day, with a little rain', 'some bright sun, but a troublesome wind' which seemed small coinage and not much in the way of discovery. But the words, 'Contrary to what I believe is the general impression, I am not in truth by nature light of heart' caught her eye and she read on with deeper interest.

Chapter 2
Isabel – 1881

July

It has been a disappointing day. I had hoped for some sun and a picnic for Marigold and Rebecca, but during the night I heard the increasing roar of the sea and by morning the sky was overcast and waves came in hungrily towards the shore as if they would devour it. There was scarce any colour anywhere, unless it was the white of the foam. Marigold (almost six years old now) was loud in disappointment, and Nanny couldn't quiet her. (Nanny – Jean Corby – is a good Scotswoman in her forties, but knows nothing about children. I have told Alexander this, but he insists she remain because of her 'integrity'. I have tried to explain that integrity is only a small portion of what is needed to care for a child, but he motions this aside.) I know how to quiet Marigold. Ah! Maybe that sounds very arrogant, but I speak no more than the truth. It's foolish, it seems to me, to decry yourself without reason. I told Marigold that if I could control the weather for her sake I would do so because I loved her and she had been (for forty-eight hours at least) a pleasant and charming child. But I could not, so we would have to do something else while we waited for it to clear up. This she accepted. Rebecca (now four) looked tearful for a moment, but made no fuss. She has a strangely adult approach to misfortune which at times I find disturbing. Perhaps the child I now carry, expected at the end of summer, will be more, as you might say, run-of-the-mill. Rebecca will never be that, though I often wonder what she will be. It's true that I love her best, most best, but I must try not to let that show. I

9

try, but perhaps I do not succeed. Love is hard, immalleable, it will not be dissimulated...

I have let a few days go by. There is no need to write every day for one day in summer is very like another. I don't complain. I love the island, I love the bay at Freshwater: I am always sad when we have to pile our luggage on to the coach and set out for Yarmouth and the ferry and at last return to London. I think of the island as my home. When we first arrive, when I see from the ferry the shape of High Down coming nearer, I feel my heart lift. That seems strange because contrary to what I believe is the general impression, I am not in truth by nature light of heart. Perhaps if I go on writing, the reason for this will become clear. Or perhaps it is just something built into me. One cannot know for certain. I have not much time for certainty – I know my dear Alexander finds this hard to accept, for he is always sure of his opinions, sure of his world. And indeed of the next, for he once said to me, 'My dear Isabel, of course there is a God; there is heaven and hell. We are told so.'

I said nothing, but perhaps my doubt showed on my face (I have never found it easy to disguise my feelings) as he went on, 'Oh my dear child, you have much to learn. But I shall teach you.' (He often calls me 'child' though he is but five years the elder. When I write it, the word sounds affectionate, but somehow, spoken, it does not. I don't know why.)

At the time of writing, Marigold, Rebecca, Nanny and I are all at Rosecroft on the island, the house that looks towards the bay on one side and the sweep of High Down on the other. We rent the house for the summer. I don't know how much that costs, for Alexander never talks to me about money. 'You don't need to worry your pretty head about that,' he would say. Sometimes it worries me that Alexander speaks in phrases that I consider outworn, but I do not dwell on it. Alexander is not greatly interested in words, or how they are put together. That I suppose is why he is – shall I say impatient? – with my great liking for poetry.

I do not know where this comes from. Neither my mother nor my father as I recall had much time for it. But from an early age I loved the metre and the rhyme, and when I discovered that here on the island we lived near to the home of Mr Alfred Tennyson, I read with passion.

One day Alexander found me reading and took the book from me. He read aloud one of my favourite lines – 'Now sleeps the crimson petal, now the white. . .' and then tossed the book down, saying, 'Pah! What awful nonsense! How can a petal sleep?'

I felt then a sudden surge of anger which quite alarmed me, for it was unaccustomed. My hands trembled, but I said only, 'It is a poem, Alexander. By Mr Tennyson.'

'I see that by the title page. A man who lives not a mile away, and about whom there is much gossip —'

'I am not interested in gossip.'

'— about the way he drinks: a bottle of port at a sitting, and smokes as if he were curing herrings.'

Indeed, I had heard something of this myself, but I did not want to dwell on it. I have no liking for drink or tobacco, and the image of such a man, clouded as it were with both, distressed me. I was ashamed that the tears came to my eyes and afraid that Alexander might see them, for the reaction was surely excessive. But whether from kindness or inattention, he turned away and said no more.

It is important – since this is a kind of confession, if only for myself – to make it clear that Alexander and I are not unhappy. He loves me, I am sure of that, and I love him. He is my husband, a man of quite exceptional presence, dark with a glisten of hair and skin, and even a kind of darkness of voice that commands attention. I have seen the women look at him and I have thought, yes, but he is *mine*, my husband. I have felt proud. For though I have my share of looks – blonde, a pale skin, triangular shape of face with grey eyes – I do not stand out in a crowd; there are many women of greater allure. Yet Alexander fell in love with me, to everyone's surprise, including mine.

I repeat, we are not unhappy. (Another poet comes to mind, who said that the lady doth protest too much. But I don't think that is so.) I am writing the truth as far as I can see it on this day of July, when the clouds that earlier cast a mantle of shadow over the bay have lifted, and there is promise of heat to come.

11

Yes, I say to Marigold, today we are going on a picnic; yes, you can bathe in the sea. Marigold jumps up and down. Rebecca grows pink and wide-eyed, as if the excitement were too great for speech. I long to put my arms round her, as if to protect her. I do not know from what. But I do not, for I must control my love. I am not sure why this is so, but I am aware of it.

So we set off. Alexander of course was not with us; he cannot take holidays as we can, his work keeps him in London. He is a solicitor – as I understand it, of some substance. He comes and goes to and from the island a little mysteriously, sometimes without warning. That is his way; he enjoys not explaining himself, not predicting his movements. One must accept that; it is his nature.

I write this at the end of the day. We took everything – basket and rug and towels and the children's bathing dresses – and walked to that point below the steep reddish sandstone cliffs where on the headland you can see Plumbley's Hotel. It is a place I am fond of – you look across the bay to the Arch rock. On the beach below the Albion Hotel (once the resort of smugglers), there are bathing machines, but I prefer this part of the shore. It is a little stony, but there is sand enough for the children. I lowered myself on to a rock where Nanny had kindly placed a cushion, so that I could sit, with my increasing bulk, in some comfort. Indeed, I was dreamily content. The sun glittered on the incoming sea and brought a strong scent of weed and salt. I watched Marigold and Rebecca as they ran to the edge of the shore and shouted as children do. I was happy there, glad to be pregnant with Alexander's third child, glad to feel the sun and smell the limitless sea.

It was just then, as I lazily turned my head, that I saw her. My first thought was that, though a stranger, she was going to speak to me, as people do on the seashore – perhaps to admire the children, for they looked pretty, laughing together at the edge of the incoming sea. But she paused for a full minute, looking at me with a curious intentness, then began to move on. Her face below the wide-brimmed hat impressed itself on me, for it was handsome – she was perhaps nearing thirty – with fine dark eyes and a tall, comely figure in its long summer dress. But there was a look in her face that disturbed me ... amusement? A kind of sardonic pity? I thought I must be imagining it, but then Nanny said, 'A stranger here. I've no' seen her before,' in that Scots tone of voice that suggests disapproval. I did not think the children had noticed her, but when she turned and walked back towards the main shore (for the great cliff prevents one going further on this strand) Marigold ran to me on bare wet sandy feet, saying, 'Mama! Mama! Who was that?'

I said, 'I don't know, darling.'

'She looked at me in a funny way. As if she knew who I was.'

Yes, that was true, but I said that she was merely interested to see little girls enjoying themselves. Rebecca said nothing, but stood, listening to us. I tried to dismiss the woman from my mind and regain that moment of timeless content, but I could not.

That night I dreamed of her, most vividly.

I never talk to Alexander about my dreams. Indeed, I know they can be tedious when spoken of. But I have sometimes known in my dreams occasions which have later come about. Nothing of great importance; I have not foreseen tragedy, or even minor misfortune. Nevertheless I have found that some circumstance, seen clearly in my dream the night before, has repeated itself the next day in real life.

Well, of course, it would be absurd to say anything of this to Alexander. If he has no time for poetry, he would have less for dreams, true or not. So I said nothing about the woman who had passed by on the shore, looked at us in a strange moment of recognition, and who later manifested herself disturbingly in my dream.

July 24th

The weather has kept fine, the children well and happy. So what is there to say? Yet I feel compelled to write; I am not quite sure why. Rebecca has been rather quieter than usual, as if absorbed in her own world, but when I ask her if she is happy, she smiles that slow smile and says, 'Yes, Rebecca is happy.'

I break off here, for on this Saturday morning there was a sudden change, the house took on noise and movement:

13

Alexander arrived. He had come in the little pony and trap from Yarmouth. As usual, he had given no warning.

He was in good spirits and looked, I thought, especially handsome, as if the sun and wind on the brief crossing had caught his skin and given it colour. The day was warm and his forehead glistened. The girls came running and he lifted them both and called them 'my chicks' and then patted them and told them to get on with their play. When they lingered (Marigold the more bold) he laughed and said, 'Ah! You think I might have brought something from London? Something of interest?' and fetched from the hall two boxes of sweets from Messrs Fortnum and Mason.

They said, 'Thank you, Papa.' They said it nicely; I didn't have to remind them.

When they had run off, Alexander put his arms round me. I caught the familiar scent of tobacco and I was glad that he had returned. I didn't ask him how long he was staying, as I know well that he doesn't like to be questioned or tied down to dates. As he looked into my face, he said, 'And how is the lovely Isabel? The mother-to-be of my son?' I made some answer, though I felt a small touch of misgiving. Alexander seems so certain that the child I carry will be a boy; he seems to have no doubts about it. 'A son!' he exclaimed once. 'How splendid it will be to have a son!'

I said after a brief pause, 'But you love the girls?'

'Why, of course,' he protested, and I thought that was true, for his eyes lightened when he greeted them, as he had just now. But he still spoke of a son, and I had no heart to remind him, as you might say, that the odds were fifty-fifty against.

When he had changed from his city clothes into the blazer and light trousers that he wore here in the bay, he poured himself a drink from the cabinet. This opened like an Aladdin's cave: the front lowered miraculously to display every kind of glass and decanter. There was a mirror at the back which increased the dazzle. I said nothing, though it did seem to me that the level in his glass was high, and that it was still early in the morning. It is best to make no comment.

However, when Alexander said, 'Oh, by the way, I've asked Beatrice to join us for luncheon,' I made a small exclamation of protest, and Alexander immediately raised his eyebrows. I said that we usually had luncheon alone when he first arrived. I did not add that I found it a little hurtful that he had made an arrangement with Beatrice before he had warned me of his arrival.

Beatrice is Alexander's sister. She is two years older, widowed early, without children, and looks on him as a god. Ah! Perhaps I have betrayed something in saying that. It became clear to me early in our marriage – indeed, even before – that Beatrice didn't count me worthy of Alexander. Perhaps she would have preferred him not to marry, for their relationship is close: they speak the same language. But if he had to marry, she would have liked ... what? I think perhaps a young woman of rank, a titled family, or – better still – someone who found Beatrice herself a source of extreme fascination. This I must confess I have failed to do.

She has something of his dark good looks. She is a prominent figure in the local church, in the drawing rooms, much admired and spoken of. Perhaps I am jealous? Both Beatrice and I try to make the best of a situation which will never be an easy one.

We had luncheon in the dining room, with the children. This was, as I feared it might be, a disaster. A quiet one, but a disaster, all the same. Marigold kept looking from the window where the sun blazed on the beckoning sea; when spoken to she answered with her head down. Rebecca sat pink and silent, wide-eyed with the longing to be somewhere else. Beatrice went on speaking in her strong upward voice, as if nothing were at odds.

When the meal was over, we sat in the garden. As far as the children were concerned, this was a little better, but not much. Marigold had changed from being silent and sulky to lively and somewhat aggressively talkative. At one point she stood in front of Beatrice and said, 'Have you brought me a present, Auntie Bea?'

This was, you might say, a double-barrelled faux pas, for if there was one thing that Beatrice disliked more than children asking for presents, it was being called 'Auntie Bea'. I saw Alexander raise his eyebrows, but he said nothing, for it was not his habit to rebuke the children in public, whether they deserved it or not. Beatrice gave a chilled smile and said, 'I'm

15

afraid little girls must wait until Christmas and birthdays for presents.' Marigold lingered, and I prayed that she wouldn't say more. Fortunately she seemed to know when she had met her match, gave an accepting nod, and wandered away.

I watched her go. If Beatrice expected some sort of apology, I didn't accommodate her. I would speak to Marigold later and tell her what she knows perfectly well – that you don't ask people (especially not Aunt Beatrice, as she likes to be called) for presents. But for the moment I would let the small uncomfortable event die in the sunny garden. Beatrice acknowledged a truce, and asked me when the 'little boy' was due. She seems as certain as Alexander that the child will be a boy. Or perhaps she simply says it to please him, which is what she mostly wants to do.

I told her, and added that I felt very well: it had been a much easier pregnancy than the other two – especially Rebecca, when I had been very sick.

'And yet,' Beatrice said, 'she is your favourite, is she not?'

Yes, naturally Beatrice would be aware of those things which I wanted to keep to myself, but I merely laughed and said, 'Oh, I love both my children.'

'We are a devoted family,' Alexander said, rising from his chair, and I took this as a sign (which it always was) that he wished to spend time with Beatrice alone. So I rose with some difficulty and prepared to go to rest, while Nanny could at last take the children to the shore.

As I lay on the wide bed I could just hear the sound of voices – the dim bass murmur of Alexander's, the lighter tone of Beatrice. Drowsily I wondered, as I sometimes did, why they had so much to say to each other. I have never asked. They are close companions and Beatrice sees me as a disappointment – though one which now she can do nothing to amend, for her principles are high and she would recoil from the idea of a broken marriage. But I cannot think they spend their time recounting my shortcomings. I don't believe that is Alexander's way. Beatrice is another matter: her tongue is sharp, one can see her taste the pleasure in the story of a failure here, a lack of courtesy there.

But, I remind myself, I have to remember that she has known shock and sorrow – that young husband, dead suddenly in his thirties of a brain haemorrhage, entirely unexpected while they were on holiday abroad, in Venice. A terrible home-coming; the bleak territory of widowhood, and no child to show a consoling likeness to his father. I had not known him, and Beatrice did not talk of him. If she had photographs, there were none on display. If she had offers of remarriage, she did not take them. She devoted herself to the Church, and to Alexander.

I lay there, growing drowsier with the afternoon. Their voices went on.

July 25th

A fine, blowy day. The sea strong, but full of light, the spray lifting on the rocks as the tide comes to the full. I found that my mind still centred on Beatrice, and it suddenly occurred to me that in some way she resembled the woman who had appeared on the shore and looked with such interest at me and the children. I thought that they seemed to be the same kind of woman. This is the sort of thing Alexander would have no time for. How can you possibly know? he would ask. A stranger seen once at the sea's edge? And I would have no answer for him, or none that he would be satisfied with.

We took our picnic today on the slope of Afton Down, for Alexander was joining us and he preferred this side of the bay. Certainly, sitting here, high on the close-cropped grass, you could see the total shape of the bay, the great bite made by the ravenous seas, the chalk cliffs, the redoubt built to counter invasion from the French. I have read somewhere that the chalk cliffs are perhaps eighty million years old, and this great gulf of time makes me a little dizzy and also afraid, for one's short life can only be a speck of time, and love and delight and sorrow as frail and of as little importance as the gulls' feathers that drift here on the wind.

But then Marigold came up to me with a small bunch of flowers which she had gathered – vetch, clover, cow parsley – and I thought the present time had meaning after all. She sometimes does things like this, and I warm to her. She is a pretty child, with her reddish hair and turned-up nose and, though wayward at times and indeed difficult to handle, has warmth and charm. She handed me the flowers and said,

17

'These are for you, Mama. I like you better than Auntie Bea. I don't like Auntie Bea.'

I laughed and hugged her. 'You mustn't call her Auntie Bea; she doesn't like it.'

'Why not?'

'I really don't know. It doesn't sound dignified enough, I suppose.'

As she wandered away, I saw Alexander coming towards me. He wore his blazer and light flannels and boater, and commanded attention, there in the bright sea-light against the sky. He seemed to me to be walking very close to the edge – there looked to be only a narrow footpace between him and the steep fall of cliff. I called, 'Alexander! Be careful!' but he laughed and said that he was quite safe. I could not however forget the tragic little stone which stood further on the Down to the memory of a child who had fallen from the cliff and been killed. It was many years ago, but the words on the stone 'to a most dear and only child' always wrung my heart. Indeed, Afton Down was not my favourite place for a picnic; the shadow of that great sorrow seemed to come on the sea wind across the Down, the vetch and the short grass. At times, walking near that stone, I felt such a wave of grief that I have stood still and covered my face with my hands.

Of course, I cannot get so far now. It was something of an effort with my bulk to reach our present place, but I had a sensation of achievement, and I thought Alexander would be pleased with me.

He sat down on the grass. The children ran to him, but I saw at once that he was not in the mood for them. They perceived this too and scampered away, while Nanny made attempts to divert them. Alexander lay back on one elbow and took off his straw boater. He looked at me with an expression I couldn't quite read (though I know most of his expressions). He looked perhaps regretful, which was not his custom. I could hear the scream of the gulls and the rhythmic wash of the sea far down. Then he said, 'I have to go back to London tomorrow, I'm afraid, my dear.'

I took a fall of heart, because at this stage of my pregnancy I was glad of his presence. I said on a slight laugh, 'That's very soon! You've only just come.'

Again he looked at me with that same expression of regret – even uncertainty. This was so unusual that I said, 'Are you quite well, Alexander?'

There was another pause and again I heard the strong pulse of the sea and the light voices of the children as they shouted together. For a moment it seemed that Alexander hadn't heard me, but then he said absently, 'Oh yes, I'm quite well; I'm never ill, you know that.' Well, yes, I did; I knew that he looked on illness as something, you might say, beneath him: he hadn't time for his own, or anyone else's much, come to that. 'I have to go,' he said, and leant forward to cover my hand with his. 'I'm sorry.'

I was in truth surprised, for again it was not his custom to make demonstrative gestures in public. But I was touched and said, 'It doesn't matter. I shall be all right. I have Nanny. And you'll be down again soon?'

He was silent, playing with my hand, and then said, 'I hope so, I hope so... But I'm busy, very busy. There are problems at work. I need to be there, in town.'

I didn't ask what the problems at the solicitor's office were. He never spoke to me of his work – in the early days when I'd asked questions he'd become impatient, for of course I did not understand legal matters (perhaps not many people do) and could not comment intelligently.

I said I understood that he had to go back to London. But the day had a shadow on it; the beauty of the cliffs and the dazzling sea were dimmed.

July 31st

So Alexander has gone, and it seems to me the summer changed after that day. I am happy with the children, and though the weight of my pregnancy grows burdensome, it is not too much. But I walk with something that comes near to sadness, though I would not call it so. I have spent much time reading poetry. The quiet cadences ease me, as they always do. These and the sound of the sea, that lovely relentless surge which makes me think of the pulse of life. An everlasting life, I suppose you'd say, but I don't know that I believe in that.

There was one excitement after Alexander's leaving that I must record. We had friends who lived at Brook, the small village high on Afton Down: Bryony and Harold Cooper. He was a sailing man, though in his sixties now, as Bryony was too. The house was filled with models of ships, paintings of the sea and windows like portholes. Harold talked with enthusiasm about ships and sailing, and I listened with fascinated attention because of my love for the sea, but Alexander grew impatient, so I was usually invited when I was alone. On this day they sent a small closed carriage to fetch me for luncheon. I went by myself; the children stayed with Nanny. Bryony and Harold are childless, and the house with its many knick-knacks (some valuable) is not the best place for small children.

The morning was grey, with a little light rain. The small carriage took me up the military road that ran across the Down; the bay was almost lost in mist. Bryony and Harold welcomed me, and Harold said I was 'a brave girl to set sail in my condition'. Bryony said, 'Isabel's always brave,' and I felt comfortable and cherished, and some of the weight that had lain on me since Alexander's leaving began to lift. It was as we finished our meal that I heard the drumming of the wind and the louder crash of the sea far below. The sky had darkened; Bryony lit the lamp on the table, so that we sat in a little circle of light. She is a woman of calm movements and I was just reflecting that I admired this when the boom of a gun made us all start, lifting our heads.

'The lifeboat!' Harold exclaimed. 'Someone must be in trouble.'

From their window it was possible to see dimly in an angry sea the small sails of a ship, plunging like a frightened horse. While we watched, a flare painted a crimson streak in the gloom; a distress signal. I stayed at the window, absorbed, until Harold said, 'Come. There is a small shelter at the end of the garden; you can see them go out. It's a great sight.'

Bryony made some sort of protest, but he waved this aside. And it was true, from the small wooden shelter we could watch the assembling of the men, their bulky life jackets shining in the gloom. 'The farmers will bring their horses,' Harold said. 'They pull the boat down the slipway and out to the launch. But it takes time.'

Perhaps it did. I sat there in the small shelter, my coat wrapped about me, totally given to this attempt at rescue. I

could see figures running in the murky and dangerous afternoon, and I felt within me that great longing for triumph, for
the saving of life. Voices came to me now, men's voices, loud
with purpose. I could see a gleam on the flanks of the horses.
Then there was a wild sound as the lifeboat moved down the
slipway, and I could hear cheers and shouts from the shore.
Harold was explaining that the launch was of the greatest difficulty, but his voice went by me, I heard and did not hear it. I
was somehow with those men in the lifeboat, and with the
sailor (whoever he was) on the small plunging craft. I was taut
with the hope of recovery; as the men pulled on their oars I
could feel within myself the strain of their effort in the heavy
run of the sea.

The wind blew more strongly, but now the lifeboat had come
close to the small sea-battered craft. 'They've reached them,'
Harold said. 'Come back to the house; I'll go down to the
shore.'

I was reluctant to leave the shelter, but it was growing colder
and Bryony brought me back inside. Waiting for Harold, I
moved to the window, seeing in my mind's eye the return of the
lifeboat, the men in their life jackets, soaked and exhausted
after their exertion. I don't know how long it was before
Harold returned. He came into the house, his face coloured,
rain gleaming on his hair and beard. He came with a kind of
triumph, there in the dark afternoon. 'They're safe,' he said.
'Two young men – foolish, they ignored weather predictions –
but they're safe. Thanks to those brave men.'

As he spoke I felt the tears come to my eyes; it seemed as
great a relief as if I had known them. The whole adventure
enclosed me as if I had been in some way part of it; and when
I returned home I felt strangely exhausted, emotionally
drained.

The children greeted me, noisy with excitement. 'There was
a big bang, Mama; Nanny says it was the lifeboat. And a light
went up from the sea. Did you see it, Mama? Did you see it?'
Marigold's eyes were bright, but I only answered her absently,
'Yes, darling, I saw it.' I could see that they were disappointed
that I was not meeting their enthusiasm. But in truth I was still
with the men in the lifeboat, and with the others on the frail
craft, so near to drowning in that angry sea.

21

That night I dreamed of limp figures lifted on to the shore, the men in their life jackets standing about them.

But they had been safe, Harold said.

September 15th
London again. A day of early autumn sunlight, mist on the trees in the Square. I should not write with so heavy a heart. But I had such a strong sense of loss on leaving the island, greater than any I have known. Nanny said, 'There, there, ma'am, we shall come back next year. With the new little one.' True, but as the trap drove away from Rosecroft with all our luggage, I had an absurd longing to stop everything and turn back to the cliffs and the sea.

September 20th
Now life is taking its London pattern. Alexander leaves after breakfast and returns at varying times later in the day. Often he seems abstracted, but I am used to that. Sometimes he is silent; I have known him say no more than a word of greeting for almost an hour. At other times he shows concern for my advancing pregnancy; he looks at me with a kind of love, even anxiety. But the doctor has told me that I am well, and that the birth should be 'straightforward'. I am not one to consider anything likely to be straightforward, but I show pleasure, and wait.

October 31st
Well, it is over now. At half past eight in the morning of the second, after some difficult hours of labour, I gave birth to a girl. She cried, and I held her in my arms. Alexander could not hide his disappointment. We have called her Sylvia. It is autumn now, the leaves mostly fallen, the skies cloudy and full of rain. I wonder how it is on the island – strong seas and the gulls flying inland. But I would be glad to be there. I want to go back, to be free of this London house where there is a shadow.

Chapter 3
Kate and Perdita – 1940

Kate looked up from the page, the faded ink. For this moment, the distant past so absorbed her that it was as if she herself was living that life, close to the island shore, giving birth in the London house. It was this wartime room and the sound of anti-aircraft fire which seemed not quite real, as if she had strayed into an alien time. More vivid was the young Isabel with her children, the images of Alexander and of Beatrice. Great Aunt Beatrice who had died some years ago in her seventies, and who had given away no secrets.

For secrets, clearly, there were. Kate had little memory of Alexander, but his figure seemed to grow tall from the pages of the book and cast a long shadow. Grandmother Isabel had said once, 'He was a good father.' But she had said it sadly.

A good father. Kate rose and poured herself a drink. She did not want for the moment to dwell on the questions which stayed unanswered in this time after Charles' death. For this moment she wanted to stay enclosed in the vivid past. The past where her mother, Marigold, was a child, playing on the shore. Suppose one could see all people as children...? Perhaps, Kate thought, one would have greater pity. Marigold, whose husband, Conrad Lewis, had left the home when Kate was five. Marigold who had, thereafter, gone down, as it were, in a mass of unpaid bills and expressions of protest at the way things were. Oh God, Kate thought, my poor mum.

And then there was Aunt Sylvia. 'We have called her Sylvia,' Isabel had written after the birth, all those years ago. Aunt Sylvia, widowed in the First World War, left with her small daughter, Perdita. Perdita, who was just now somewhere in the

23

dangerous London streets. I'd like her back, Kate thought, taking steps across the room, glass in hand. Not many people I want to see at this time, but Perdita is one. Shall I tell her? About me? Not yet, I don't think... But there's not much time.

A long sound of the doorbell. Had it rung more than once? Acknowledging at least one stroke of good fortune, Kate opened the door to her younger cousin. 'Sorry,' she said, 'lost in thought. Come and get warm.'

Perdita came into the hall, wrapped against the cold with woollen scarf and woollen hat. She might be any age, Kate thought, from sixteen to twenty-five. Stamping her feet on the mat she pulled off the woollen cap to show reddish hair cut short and a face whose skin had been whipped by the wind. Kate thought it was an engaging face, not beautiful, but eager, large-eyed, mouth a little way open, ready to gasp in astonishment or exclaim in admiration. A trace of Isabel there, Grandmother brought up to date? It was somehow a courageous face; you could see her going ahead, unwisely perhaps, with a banner like Joan of Arc.

'I was beginning to worry,' Kate said.

'Gosh,' said Perdita, 'about me? Being blown up? Don't think it's likely – the odds, I believe, are against it.' She gave Kate a crooked smile, but didn't mention Charles. Didn't look abashed either. She was not, Kate reflected, trying to apologise or to cheer her, she was not trying to do anything. She was like an obedient child, ready to be told what is going to happen next, a wise child who will not ask silly questions.

'Are you scared?' Kate asked, as they came into the small, curtained living room.

Perdita, pulling off coat and scarf and suddenly looking much smaller, said, 'Well, *kind* of. And yet in a way not, for it's out of one's hands... Oh!' she exclaimed. 'You found it – the box! Oh, well done.'

One might have scored a goal on the playing field, Kate thought affectionately. She showed Perdita the journals, the shabby books sliding together, and told her something of what she had so far learned. Perdita, taking one of the books and turning the pages, said, 'I can't wait to know ... do they all come into it? Grandfather Alex? And our mums? And the others? All of it written down ... what a find.'

24

Yes, Kate thought, Perdita wouldn't fail as a fellow explorer. 'Are you,' she said, 'too tired to come out to eat? Pub round the corner?'

No, Perdita said, she wasn't too tired. This was not the kind of day when one gets tired; it just seems to go on and on. Like the war.

Both now wrapped against the cold, they went out into the unlighted street. More as talismen than protection, they took gas masks in cardboard boxes. The all clear had not sounded, but the anti-aircraft fire had quietened. Cloud covered the moon, the bombers' moon. Here and there a little spurt of light grew and died as a passer-by struck a match; voices were disembodied, mysterious, laughter came lightly, vanishing in the dark. Perdita, hands in her pockets, talked confidingly about her day. She had been to visit her mother, Sylvia Lord (née St Clair) who was cared for in a home outside Watford. Her mind was in some confusion, but she occasionally took cartridge paper and charcoal (or was given it) and drew with skill and surprising power.

'How did it go?' Kate asked, for she had known Aunt Sylvia through the difficult sad years, and Perdita said it went like it always did. You were torn between pity and a desire to be gone. You don't like yourself much because of the desire to be gone. It's like being in a room with no doors – there's no good way out; you can't make it all right. Like the war. Like most of life, perhaps.

'After Mum,' Perdita said, 'I went to see an old school friend – poor lamb, her husband's a prisoner of war, taken at Dunkirk. She is, to be honest, not a very bright girl, but she somehow became my friend, my close friend. They say you choose your friends, but I don't think that's always so, do you? They just seem to *happen*. And now she's there alone with a baby, and afraid her husband won't come back. And of course I can't promise her that he will, because no one can promise anything just now, and it's silly to try.'

'You seem to have had a pretty exhausting day,' Kate observed, and Perdita said it would be hard just now to think of anyone who hadn't had an exhausting day.

And that, Kate thought, is why I find Perdita restful company; she is never sorry for herself. Come to think of it, perhaps she gets that too from Isabel.

25

The pub received them with warmth and sudden light, the scent of cigarette smoke and the cameraderie of people who have cheerfully so far escaped a common danger.

'Beer and sausages, if I can get them?' Kate asked, and Perdita said that would be wonderful; as if, Kate thought, she'd been offered caviar. Caviar, however, would be out in any case, since no meal must cost more than five shillings.

Enclosed by the sound of many voices, Kate sat opposite Perdita, with the beer and sausages before them, and showed her the photograph of Alexander and Isabel and their children. 'Thought you'd like to see this,' Kate said.

'Gosh, *yes*,' Perdita said. 'But I believe I've seen it before – in Grandmother's room, perhaps? Didn't someone say it was taken by Julia Margaret Cameron?'

'Yes, indeed; but it couldn't have been, the dates don't fit. People always want things to be more exciting than they really are.'

'So they do,' said Perdita on a sigh, as if she regretted it. 'There's Mum – and your mother. They look so pretty.'

Pleasing, Kate found, to go over the shared past; to talk of Marigold, her mother – the disastrous marriage, and all the subsequent unpaid bills. But Marigold had still been pretty and with enough charm to keep her in 'admirers' (lovers, maybe), though she never married again. She just wrote postdated cheques which, when the date came, had to be postdated again... And then there was the cancer, quite sudden: Marigold, poor love – what was the word? – bewildered, perhaps, not able to understand how all the taxis and the nice meals and the kind gentlemen who gave admiration and loving words, but never really stayed long enough to propose, were no good any more, because it was all coming to an end. Yet *there*, in this photograph, was the little girl who brought flowers to Isabel on the edge of the Down, with the sea far below.

'She brought flowers?' Perdita said.

'It's all in the journal.'

'What else?'

'I don't know,' said Kate. 'There's more. A lot more.'

Into the crowded place with its voices and cigarette smoke, the level trumpet-note of the all clear sounded and some of the heads lifted in brief recognition. A man said over his beer,

26

'Don't count on it; they'll be back. The night's still young.' From outside came the clang of rescue lorries, the wail of ambulance sirens. Kate looked aside; the sounds woke the echo of that other raid, and for a moment she covered her eyes with her hand.

'You OK?' Perdita asked. 'We can go home, if you like.'

Kate shook her head. 'Sorry. It comes on suddenly, like toothache.'

'I expect that's just what it's like,' said Perdita with sympathy, but not too much. 'I've never – oh God, touch wood – lost anyone I loved. I'm frightened for Gerald, of course, flying in that bloody plane – sometimes very frightened. But I have an odd feeling that he'll come through. Wild optimism? Or sixth sense? Grandmother Isabel had a sixth sense.'

Again Kate looked aside. 'I can remember her when she was very old, telling our fortunes – how much did she see, d'you think? You and Gerald; me and Charles on the island, perhaps?'

Perdita sat with her chin on her hands. 'Why is that comforting?'

Kate drank from her glass. 'Because it does something to time. It's time we're afraid of – I remember reading, 'O let not Time deceive you; you cannot conquer time'. But if you *can* ... if it's not what we believe ... am I making sense?'

'No,' said Perdita, 'but I like what you say. Go on.'

'When Grandmother lived on the island, Tennyson was still alive, not a mile away; Browning and Matthew Arnold were still living. But Charles and I used to visit Farringford, and Charles liked the little iron staircase where Tennyson used to escape from people he didn't want to see ... maybe she saw more than we knew.'

Perdita looked thoughtful, then said, 'At the funeral, there was that man. The stranger – perhaps sixty or more. He must have known her, else why was he there?'

Kate nodded. 'He looked at us as if he knew us, yet he never spoke. Why, d'you think?'

'People behave oddly at funerals. They are, after all, pretty strange events. *They* don't belong to time. A point where mystery meets the commonplace facts. Rather good that, eh?'

'Perhaps he'll come back,' Kate said. 'After all, he found

out about the funeral. He hadn't just drifted in off the street. He's part of it, somehow.'

'So,' Perdita said, draining her glass, 'there's more to learn... Ready now?'

As they left the pub and met the dark street once more, Kate said suddenly, 'I'd like to go back to the island. Not as it is now, full of troops, with the beaches a mass of concrete and barbed wire. But as it was ... quiet, with all those great names and its secrets.'

Perdita took her arm. 'She wrote it all down,' she said. 'For you, perhaps?'

Chapter 4
Isabel – 1885

August

I have not written for some time, but on this morning when, after a hazy start, the sun has brought families to the edge of the sea, I feel moved to pick up my pen once more. There is much to record, but I must begin with that event which changed our family – the birth of Toby.

Yes! Alexander has his son. Toby was born twelve months ago, a lovely boy with large grey eyes set far apart and a slow smile. (He can also cry for what seems like hours with fury, but I know how to quiet him in the end.) Alexander was in high spirits that evening of Toby's birth. He might have been a king who'd achieved a longed-for heir. I can see him standing at the end of my bed, glass in hand, lamplight on his skin, on his hair, on the liquid in his glass, tall with triumph. 'So you see, my dearest, I was right after all. We have a son!' Drowsy after the birth, I looked at him with mingled pleasure and misgiving. Why misgiving? My mind still blurred with exhaustion, I couldn't find the right words ... perhaps, standing there, he seemed to give out power, too much power. Perhaps a kind of shadow seemed to fall across his joy, of which he was unaware. Or perhaps, behind his joy, there were words unspoken... But then I told myself that was nonsense; there could be nothing of importance which Alexander needed to tell me.

Yes, he was delighted with his son. It was he who chose the name – Tobias, after the son of Tobit in the book of the Apocrypha. He became 'Toby' very quickly, of course, and remains so. Alexander always had a great feeling for the books of the Apocrypha: Ecclesiasticus, Judith, the first and second

29

books of the Maccabees. These were but names to me – familiar names, no more. I preferred poetry to the Bible, though I found beauty in the psalms. But Alexander, having no time for poetry, read the Bible with devout attention and said it was better than anything that Mr Tennyson (or Lord Tennyson, as he had lately become) or Mr Browning could compose.

I have to say – since this is a private journal, I may say it – that I am relieved that my last child was the boy Alexander longed for. Of course I expect our marital relations will continue, for Alexander is still a young man – but there has always been something ... what is the word, is 'brutal' too strong? ... in his lovemaking. I have not of course mentioned this to anyone. Perhaps if I had a sister – but I am an only child. So it is a secret I have had to keep.

I am not a woman of narrow emotions, I know what love and desire mean, and I have loved Alexander. But it is strange how he can change from a man of manners and courtesy to something quite other in our marriage bed – someone not given to loving words, not to gentleness of any kind. A violence, as if this were in some way a battle where he had to overcome, not a lovemaking. I knew no pleasure in it. I should have done – but I did not. I never spoke to him of this, and he never asked, merely turned aside with a grunt of exhaustion and slept. The next day he would be his usual self – always with that sense of power, but showing an occasional gentleness, a glance of approval, an intimacy of laughter. Almost he might have been a different man, as if the night had never happened. Sometimes I wondered if these courtesies – even intimacies – were an unspoken apology, for one cannot know another person's mind. But I do not think he apologised.

So on this morning, while the sun strengthened on the sea, we were together – except for Alexander – at Rosecroft. As I moved from the breakfast table I thought, after all, that I was a fortunate woman. I had four children, three girls and the son Alexander always wanted. Marigold and Sylvia were in the garden, Toby was in his high chair and Rebecca was still sitting at the table, lost in a dream. But Rebecca was often quiet.

'Rebecca wasn't a very good girl in the night,' Nanny said. 'Calling for glasses of water at all hours.'

I said only, 'Well, I expect she was thirsty.' Nanny pursed her lips but said no more.

Yes, I thought – accepting without protest Nanny's view that I favoured Rebecca – yes, I was lucky. And then, as the girls' voices clamoured from the garden, there came to my mind unbidden the image of the woman who had so long ago turned to look at us on the familiar shore. The tall handsome woman who had managed to convey intimacy and scorn at the same time. I had not seen her since. Or – I don't think I had. Once or twice in the quiet lanes of Freshwater I thought I caught sight of a tall figure which reminded me of her, but I could not be sure. After all, I had only seen her that once. But it had been enough to convince me that she was not a happy woman. She did not, as I had just done, consider herself fortunate. I don't know how I was sure of this, but I was. Indeed, so great an impression had that brief encounter made on me that I sometimes dreamed of her. In my dreams there was some kind of anger between us; I would wake from them, disturbed, as if I had to brush my way through cobwebs into the sunlight.

But she did not appear again on the shore.

Quickly on that morning my sense of good fortune revived and I helped Nanny prepare the children for the day. Rebecca showed signs of wanting to stay at home. This was so unusual that I asked her if she was feeling ill. She seemed to ponder this, then said, no, it wasn't that. Pressed further, she would say no more.

But before we could set out, Beatrice, Alexander's sister, arrived. I found this entirely unexpected. She was not a regular visitor – she only came as a rule when Alexander was with us. She wore light clothes, a pretty dress of lilac colour, a large hat with the same coloured ribbon, and she carried a lilac parasol. I felt a little drab beside her. She seemed in cheerful mood and able to ignore the fact that her presence had cast a shadow on the children – all, that is, except Toby, who, unconcerned, gave out crowing noises of pleasure.

'I have brought some special cakes,' Beatrice said, displaying a light basket. 'Martha' – Martha was her cook '– has just made them, and I thought they would be excellent for hungry little mouths by the seashore.'

I don't know why Beatrice always talked like that, and why

31

it set my teeth on edge. Perhaps because it didn't ring true – she didn't in fact greatly care for the children, and 'hungry little mouths' was a phrase used to cover up her natural antipathy. However, I took this at its face value, and we all set off: Nanny and the children (Toby in his baby carriage), Beatrice and I walking together, heads bent in conversation. To any passing stranger we must have appeared to be women friends pleased to have time to ourselves. But then I suppose all of us look content enough to those outside.

Beatrice decided that we should sit on the other part of the shore, not the stretch which I always favoured. But I made no protest, not because I cannot stand up to Beatrice, but because it was too trivial a matter to make a fuss about. Beatrice looked back at my favourite shore and said, 'It is that large rock. I don't like it. At low tide it stands up like a great table, a place for a sacrifice.' I was startled by this, for it wasn't the way that Beatrice usually spoke or, I would have thought, imagined. I looked across at the rock, and indeed at low tide it did stand up with a certain menace. I turned away.

We settled on the main shore, a little distance from the bathing machines. Nanny fussed about (she was always at her most fussy when Beatrice was present); the children lost their inhibitions in the open air, with the boisterous, shining sea close to their feet and the shouts of other children nearby. As always, the nearness of the sea quietened me; I thought I could watch it for ever. And then Beatrice mentioned a friend of hers, a man who had retired to the island from London, but then suddenly died. 'So sad,' Beatrice said, turning her parasol. 'A widower of sixty-five; he had so much to give to life.'

I did for a moment wonder if part of what he had to give to life was an offer of marriage to Beatrice, but then Sylvia, who was close by, picked up a pebble and said, 'It doesn't really matter when people die, does it?'

As she turned away to join her sisters, Beatrice said, 'What an extraordinary child.'

'Most children are extraordinary,' I said. 'Adults too, come to that. But usually they learn to disguise it.' I spoke equably, but my heart accelerated, for in truth I was aware of an occasional oddity in Sylvia's behaviour – extreme swings of mood,

32

from sweetness to anger; at other times a total detachment, as if nothing had any importance for her. Nanny had coined a phrase – 'It's that Miss Sylvia again' – which affected me as I suppose it would affect most mothers: I rallied to Sylvia's defence. As I had just now.

When she had decided to take this as a joke (though I could see that she did not truly perceive it so) Beatrice said, again moving her parasol, 'I have some news for you, Isabel dear.'

'News?'

'Alexander wants you to join him for a short time in London.'

'To join him in *London*?'

'Well, really, Isabel, I don't think you need to sound so surprised! You are his wife, after all, and if he wants you to be with him, it's surely natural enough that you should go.'

I didn't answer at once, but looked aside to the glittering sea and the children playing at its edge. I couldn't argue with that, but nor could I explain that it was against the natural order of things – and in some way disturbing – that Alexander should want me to join him in London. He simply never did. So why now? It was true, of course, that I didn't want to go. I was content here – no, more than content. I was always prepared for Alexander's visits, however unheralded, and I would adjust the pattern of my life and the children's life to suit him. I didn't expect any of this to change.

Perhaps this shows an unadventurous, not to say simple nature, but I had my love of poetry, that wild domain of the imagination. I could walk over the Downs alone with the words streaming in my head, the plunge and glitter of the sea far below seeming to echo them. I would look across to the house where the poet lived and know that magic had been woven there. Up there on the ridge of the Down, where the vetch and clover trembled in the sea wind, I would sometimes feel a sensation that was beyond happiness or sorrow, in some way beyond time. I could tell no one of this, least of all Alexander or Beatrice, which is why I find it necessary to write it down.

'Indeed,' I said to Beatrice, 'I have always tried to do what Alexander wants of me. But he has always said that London in the summer is not good for me or the children.'

Beatrice lifted her head: I had the sense that she was

33

uncertain what next to say. Marigold and Rebecca ran to me, bringing a piece of seaweed. Beatrice glanced briefly at them, but did not, I think, really see them. 'Of course,' she said, 'there would be no question of the children going with you.'

Well, naturally, I said, I wouldn't expect to uproot the children from the island and take them to London in mid-summer – what would they do there?

Before I could speak Marigold said, 'Are you going away, Mama?' and Rebecca said, 'Don't go, Mama. Stay with us.' I drew a hand over their heads and told them to join Nanny, Sylvia and Toby. When they'd gone I asked Beatrice why Alexander had not put this to me himself. She adjusted a fold of her skirt. 'I have just come back from London,' she said. 'I saw Alexander: he asked me to give you the message.'

'Just that?' I said. 'No letter, no greeting?'

'He sent you his love.'

I thought about this. 'Sending love' is a common pastime: it can mean so much or so little. But for Alexander? He would not speak lightly; that was not his way. 'But why,' I asked, 'does he want me to go to London?'

Beatrice's brief silence seemed to suggest that as a good wife I should obey without questioning, but she said, 'It is important that you accompany him to a dinner engagement.'

'A *dinner* engagement? Why can't it wait till the autumn?'

'Really, Isabel, should I have brought this urgent message if it could?'

That was true, but it didn't answer my question. As if she perceived this, Beatrice said, 'It is a matter to do with his work.'

'His work? But he never discusses it with me; I know nothing about it. I once tried to read a legal document and it might have been written in Chinese.'

'We are not expected to understand the language of the law,' Beatrice said, and I could not help replying that this was just as well, wasn't it? 'The matter,' Beatrice went on, 'is to do with ... with the social side of his work. It is necessary for him to bring his wife to dinner with a client.'

I simply said, 'Why?'

A flicker of annoyance on her face? I thought so. She said, 'Sometimes it is necessary for a man of law to, let us say, make the right impression.'

'And I can help him to do that?'

A faint pursing of her lips. 'Alexander believes so.'

'When does he want me to go?'

'Tomorrow.'

I did not show surprise, for in a sense I felt none. This visit from Beatrice had had all along something of urgency in it. We stayed a little longer on the shore, but I thought the joy had gone out of it. I was glad when Beatrice rose and said that she must return home. I offered to walk with her, but she refused, saying that I would need time to prepare for my journey the next day.

This was true, and we soon returned from the shore. The children were fretful, tired perhaps from the sun. Nanny's voice took on a Scottish sharpness, and Sylvia made a face behind her back. Marigold said she was bored and Toby started to cry. Rebecca was silent, rubbing her neck. I asked her what was the matter and she said she had a sore throat. I glanced at Nanny, who shook her head. 'The wee girl always says she has a sore throat: it's a phase she's picked up.' ('Phase' is Nanny's word for 'phrase'.)

'Really a sore throat?' I asked, but Rebecca stayed silent, looking at me with tear-filled eyes.

At last she said, 'Don't want you to go away.' The other children (except Toby of course, who just went on crying) took this up. 'Please, Mama! Don't go away. Stay here.' Marigold and Sylvia were making a good deal of noise, Marigold shouting, 'Don't go! Don't go!' and Sylvia trying to outdo her, almost screaming (for Sylvia always had to go to the limits) until I lost my temper and told them to be quiet.

I had spoken so sharply that Toby cried more loudly, but the others obeyed me, going silently with their heads down. Nanny gave me a glance of approval, but I did not like my anger, and when later they came down in their dressing gowns to kiss me goodnight, I hugged them with sudden strength. I felt as I embraced them a painful twist of the heart, as if I were saying goodbye to them for a long while. As I watched them go up to bed, hair brushed, heads still bent, I had a powerful longing to gather them all together in one protective movement, to cast some spell on them which would make their future safe. But that of course was impossible; no one has those sort of powers.

35

When they were all in bed and asleep, I went out of the house. Yes, I had to prepare for my journey the next day but, just for this moment, I needed to walk alone on the familiar path above the sea. The sun was low, defining the cliff faces in the colour of apricot, the tide ebbing, so that I could see the wet darkened shore and the green-weeded rocks far down. I walked vigorously; light showed too on the undersides of the gulls as they flew, crying harshly, inland. I could see the poet's house, and the house called Dimbola where the woman photographer had lived. Echoes were on the air, of the poetry I read, of the names of great men who visited there, of the past. The summons from Alexander still troubled me, but I tried to push it from my mind.

I stood still, there on the High Down. It was a magic hour, up there alone: the shore deserted, the colour at once rich and dying on the cliff face, the sea paling almost to white. A little breeze caught my skirt and I held it with one hand. What else touched me? The magic, perhaps? For it seemed to me that I stood in that moment outside time. I don't know how to explain it. I had not gone mad – I knew that the children slept in their beds, and Nanny was tidying their clothes. And yet I had a sensation of another place, another time. A future time? I thought so. I was aware of darkness, and sudden dangerous lights, gulfs of fire ... and then a girl, a companion. Someone close to me, yet though I knew her I could not give her a name. I couldn't see her face, but as the danger and darkness increased I seemed to be pulled away from her. I wished to call to her, but could not; I felt a kind of love for her, as I felt for my own children. But this was different, for I could not be sure of her existence; it was like crying after the dead. No – not the dead, I told myself, in a sudden shaft of knowledge. Someone who will live. Live beyond my time.

A dream? No, I was fully awake, aware of myself on the Down in the failing light. Shaken, I turned and made my way back to the house. Here and there lamps were lit, the day had almost gone. Only the last wing of sunset light lay on the cliff face and on the withdrawing tide.

Yes, the lamps were lit, the children asleep. All was as it should be. That taste of dangerous streets and a companion haunted me, but I had to prepare for my journey the next day.

August 20th

I write now, home once more on the island, after two nights in London. There was a storm in the night, but the morning is clear, the sea lazily casting wracks of seaweed on the shore. I am glad to be here in the familiar house; I woke to the sound of the sea with relief and misgiving. For the time in London has disturbed me.

I arrived at the Russell Square house in the early evening. London was grey, heavy with warmth. I could not deny that the city in summer always lowered my spirits, and I longed for the shore and the wide sea, instead of the canyons of the streets, the sound of horse carriages, a sense of being shut within walls.

But Alexander greeted me with warmth, a lightness that had a spark of gaiety: he was at his most charming. A shame, he said, to drag me from my beloved bay, but he was delighted to see me. I was surprised, for nothing Beatrice had said had prepared me for this. He put his arm round my waist as we entered the house, as if he was proud of me, though there was no one to see us except cook, who gave me her usual melancholy smile. (Cook, despite a kindly nature, takes most pleasure in death and disaster, and at the moment it seemed that Alexander and I were not providing either of these.)

I tried to question Alexander about this summons, the dinner which it was so important for me to attend, but he waved my questions away. That night he made love to me with as much gentleness as I believe he was capable of. The next day his spirits were still high. He did not speak of the evening to come, until I insisted that I must know something of what was in store for me.

Alexander was tying his black tie before the looking glass. He lifted his chin, gave a small confident smile, and said that we were meeting a lady in her later years, Mrs Duvane, and that she had been remaking her will. But how, I asked, could that possibly affect me? I know nothing about wills. Naturally not, he said. But Mr Duvane had a nephew who had been talking to her about her investments, and she had ideas about changing her lawyer. But why? I asked, and Alexander said that young men liked to throw their weight about. He, Alexander, had handled all Mrs Duvane's investments to her entire satisfaction for many years and there was no earthly reason for her to change anything or anyone.

'But *me*,' I said. 'Where do I come in? You asked me to come urgently to London, but what possible use could I be in this matter of investments?'

Alexander turned from the looking glass. 'Because, my dear, Mrs Duvane is a sentimental lady with strong views on the sanctity of family life. She had a very happy marriage, though there were sadly no children: a son died at birth. She is a deeply religious woman with a wholehearted belief in the power of a loving family. I have spoken to her of you, and of the children, and she expressed a wish to meet you. Now, no more questions, my dear. All it requires is that you should be your usual charming self, talk of the family – perhaps, if it seems to come naturally, suggest that I'm a good and loving father – that is, if you think I am!'

This was said on a laugh. Was it a comfortable laugh? I said of course I thought he was a good father. There was no time to say more, for we were now in a hurry to go down to the hansom cab which would take us to Mrs Duvane's house in South Kensington, not far from Onslow Square.

I thought it a strange evening. I had no difficulty in talking – or rather listening – to Mrs Duvane. She was a woman of about sixty, with evidence of a lost prettiness, hair mostly grey and somewhat adrift; she had a sort of childlike eagerness to which I responded. I tried, as Alexander had asked me, to talk to her about my family, but though she gave exclamations of pleasure at the children's names, she didn't really listen to anything I said, and just went on happily talking. I am fairly used to this, and am indeed surprised when anyone gives me full attention. So I listened to Mrs Duvane, to her views on the young, the Church, the importance of discipline in the family. Out of the corner of my eye I could see Alexander talking to Mrs Duvane's nephew. His name was Gilbert, and he did not at all resemble her, being dark, smooth-haired and, it seemed to me, somewhat taciturn. He sat, his eyes on Alexander, unsmiling, but – yes, I thought – listening. When he spoke he gave after his words an intense glance, as if to drive them home. Alexander did not, as far as I could see, find this disconcerting.

When the conversation became general, I thought the nephew, Gilbert, lost interest, though he made an effort to be polite, and I could just tell – though he was a good ten years younger than I – that he thought me pretty enough to give me a fractionally longer glance than was necessary. This is something which every woman, vain or not, can always I think perceive. As for Mrs Duvane, it was clear that her manner towards us had taken on a greater depth of friendliness – whether this had anything to do with my presence I couldn't know. Her nephew became, if anything, more taciturn, and towards the end of the evening had the manner of a man who can scarcely disguise the fact that he wants the whole thing to be done.

Alexander on the other hand had the sunny relief of a man who has played a hard game and won. He was at his most composed and charming, bowing over Mrs Duvane's hand as he said goodbye; giving Gilbert, the nephew, a farewell of false friendliness, which all the same had a glint of triumph. His good humour held as we returned home. 'You were splendid, my dear,' he said. 'Splendid!' I began to protest that I hadn't done very much, but he waved this aside.

When he saw me off for my return to the island, his high spirits had, I thought, lessened, as if his mind was moving away from the success of the evening before to other matters less congenial. But when I questioned him, the smile was back and he said he was in very good heart.

But yes, returned now to the island I cannot deny that the evening with Mrs Duvane had disturbed me. She and her nephew had the mysterious quality of people with whom one has been in close contact, but whom one does not expect to see again. Yes, I understood, not being a complete fool, that Alexander was anxious not to lose Mrs Duvane as a client – but was it worth bringing me up to London simply to listen to her? I would not dwell on it, I thought. I had done what he asked of me. We had been happy. I did not know when he would return to the island, but I did not dwell on this either.

In the morning early, before the children were up and about, I walked down to the shore. The tide was low, the sea quiet. Morning light showed the strange rock, standing clear of the water, draped with weed of a brilliant green. I remembered

39

how Beatrice had described it – something about an altar for sacrifice? With the plash of the incoming sea in my ears, I wondered about the age of the rock, as I had wondered about the age of the cliffs. That sea was the bed from which all life had sprung. Or so Mr Darwin, whose writing I had read, suggested, and I believed him: there is an ancient mystery in the sea. (I do not talk about Mr Darwin to Alexander, for he gets very angry. I am not quite sure why: the writings seem eminently sensible to me.)

As I turned to walk back to the house, reflecting on the brief span of life when faced with the timeless sea, I had that sudden hint of a young woman whose name I didn't know, a feature-less yet palpable person, close to me. I knew nothing of her, except that in some way I shared her future joy and sorrow, and that she would understand my love of poetry and my wonder-ings about time.

When I reached the house I found the children ready – all except Rebecca. She was a little poorly, Nanny said, and still in bed.

I went quickly upstairs, and knelt down beside Rebecca's bed. She murmured, 'Mama?' Her face was flushed, her eyes heavy. I asked her what was the matter, and she said, 'My throat hurts.'

'Badly?' I asked, and she seemed to think about this.

'No, just a bit.' Then, 'You went away. Don't go away again.'

'No, my dearest,' I said, 'I won't go.' (But I said it in the passion of the moment: at that time I had no intention of going anywhere.) I kissed her hot forehead and went downstairs to tell Nanny that one of the maids must fetch the doctor. I could see that Nanny thought this unnecessary, but I paid no atten-tion. 'She has a sore throat and a temperature,' I said. 'You take the children to the shore.'

'Yes, ma'am,' Nanny said, in a voice I knew. Marigold protested, and Sylvia joined in. 'We want you to come, Mama: come with us.' Rebecca wasn't well, I told them; I had to stay with her till the doctor came. 'Bother Rebecca,' Sylvia said, 'I don't like her: she's a nuisance.' She was shushed by Nanny.

Doctor Lang came within the hour. He was an old man, somewhat eccentric, who always seemed to wear clothes too

40

warm for the day; in this case, a cape and a cap. (He made his visits mostly on foot.) He had a manner of embracing kindliness, which rang true, and an air of certainty, which did not.

'The little one not well? Ah – we must do our best for that.' Rebecca smiled at him, for he had a way with children: he was childlike himself. He examined Rebecca and said she was indeed a little feverish, but it was no more than a bad cold. She must drink plenty of water and stay in bed for a day or two. There was nothing to worry about.

'Her throat?' I asked, but he said that was just part of the infection; he would prescribe a syrup. The discomfort would pass. I said I didn't like to see her so quiet – children should make a noise! Dr Lang put a hand on my shoulder. 'No worry, no worry, my dear! I remember my wife almost in tears one day over a child, and the next she was crying for mercy because of the noise. All will be well.'

Yes, he had comforted me. Indeed, Rebecca seemed to be somewhat restored by his visit, and by evening I could tell by her cooler forehead and her eagerness for bananas and cream (her favourite food) that she was better.

August 22nd

Two days later, as Dr Lang had prophesied, she seemed quite well again. We took our picnic to the shore and she ran to the sea's edge with delight. Marigold was being good to her, nicely playing the elder sister. She can be such a good girl, Marigold. Sometimes my heart aches when I see her being good, for I fear that there is something within her which will prevent her being happy. I do not have this feeling about Rebecca; I think she is made for happiness.

Sylvia on the other hand was still sulking because I had stayed at home. I stroked her hair and tried to ease her out of her mood. She is – if truth be told – the one who causes me the most anxiety. There is a wildness in her – a darkness, perhaps. 'Be kind to Rebecca,' I said. 'She's your sister; she's not been well.'

Sylvia kicked at the sand. 'She's a nuisance.' It was no good arguing with her in this mood. Watching her, I felt powerless, as I did with Marigold, for there is the long future which, whatever I do, and however much I love, is out of my control.

August 24th

This morning I walked with Beatrice on the Down. She was in good spirits; I was more at home with her than usual. (I reflected that our meetings were always better when the children were not with us.) She mentioned my London sojourn. 'I'm sure you enjoyed it,' she said, as if I'd gone for my own pleasure. I didn't immediately answer, and I saw her glance at me.

I said evenly, 'I found it interesting.'

'In what way, interesting?' she asked.

I explained that I did not fully understand the urgent need for my presence, and that I thought Mrs Duvane's nephew rather ... I supposed the word was, unwelcoming.

'I haven't met him,' Beatrice said, rather to my surprise, for I thought she would know more about everything to do with Alexander than I did. This sounds strange, but it is true. 'In what way unwelcoming?' she pursued.

I shrugged, growing a little tired of this. The evening after all was done. 'When we said goodbye, he looked as if he was glad to be gone.'

'He did not seem in any way elated?' she asked.

I said, 'By no means.'

She seemed to become more at ease, gave a brief sigh of relief, and began to speak of the new rector. I gave this only passing attention, for I had not Beatrice's interest in all things to do with the Church.

That is not to say that I do not have a belief of my own. But it *is* my own, and seems to have nothing to do with the social goings-on which Beatrice enjoys so much. Whatever I believed in seemed to me so vast and mysterious, so much akin to the sea I loved, deep, unfathomable, that the gossip, concern about candles, cakes and bazaars seemed to bring the whole matter down to a size too small. However, I could not imagine that the new rector, whose name was Piers Malleson, would have any time for or interest in my views. But Beatrice was still talking of him. 'He is a widower, poor man,' she said. 'His wife died in childbirth. We don't know very much more about him. There has been some talk, but I don't pay attention to rumours; I like to see for myself.'

'What kind of rumours?' I asked, without full interest.

Beatrice said, 'It seems that his sermons can sometimes be controversial.' This did rouse a faint nerve of interest, but I could not think that I would ever have occasion to discuss such matters with him.

August 26th

Such glorious weather! Each morning the sun seems to come up, dripping light from the sea, and the days are cloudless with heat: it seems that 'warm days will never cease'. (I know John Keats was writing about autumn, but those are the words which come to my mind.) What has happened of account? I have watched the children; I have visited the less fortunate on the island. Beatrice does this with determination and panache, you might say, but I cannot do it so; I feel there is something unacceptable about a woman with my advantages coming into their homes, as if from some higher sphere. Maybe they are better people than I am; it's not for me to come with gifts, say a few commonplace words, and return to my comfortable life.

We have had Marigold's tenth birthday – a special picnic and presents: a new dress (for she likes clothes) and, to her palpable disappointment, an umbrella from her aunt Beatrice. Sylvia said, 'Why isn't it *my* birthday?' but Rebecca seemed happy enough: she doesn't appear to be anxious for presents as Sylvia is. She picked some flowers on our way to the shore (only daisies and dandelions and some grass, but they looked pretty) and gave them to Sylvia to comfort her. Sylvia tossed them away, and I felt a pang (absurd, of course) but I was glad to see that Rebecca only gathered more and kept them to herself. Eight years old now, she has an odd dignity. (However, I did see her make a face at Sylvia behind her back.)

And Toby? Alexander's prized son? He is a good-tempered child (as a rule) and on meeting strangers looks at them steadily with wide grey eyes as if they posed some sort of conundrum, then – as often as not – he smiles slowly, with a touch of condescension, as if he were royalty. It is hard to believe that he will one day be a man – a man like Alexander. But one day he will be so – and for a moment the relentless passing of time touches me: the changes will come, the years fall by like leaves. What will remain? The cliffs tall above me, the sea...

I turn again to Toby as he looks with large-eyed interest at the incoming waves, and wonder what goes on in his mind. 'The whole world lies before him like a land of dreams...' Oh, yes, I know what that is: words of the poet about whom Alexander becomes most angry: Mr Matthew Arnold. The world which seems 'so beautiful, so various, so new, Hath really neither joy, nor love, nor light, Nor certitude, nor peace nor help for pain ...' Now why should I remember that while watching Toby as he stares wide-eyed at the sea?

But I must come to the strange incident which marked this day.

There were many people on the shore. I watched them with idle interest, until I turned to see a boy standing, legs apart, looking towards me. He was no more than six years old, but he drew one's eye, with his wet dark hair and his bathing dress, also wet, and an expression on his face of extreme mischief. He looked like a child who has broken all the rules and got away with it. I glanced round to see perhaps his mother or his nurse, but he seemed to stand there alone. For a moment, as our eyes met, I had the sensation that I had seen him somewhere before. I half expected him to speak to me, but after a moment he spread his thin arms wide, as if he were about to fly, then turned and ran away. I tried to see where he went, but quickly he became lost in the crowd, behind the bathing machines.

He had disturbed me. 'Did you see that boy?' I asked Nanny, but she merely said she'd seen no particular boy; there were many playing on the shore. Restless, I got to my feet, climbed the few steps to the promenade, and walked in the direction he'd gone. His looks in that moment of encounter had been so distinctive, even electrifying, that I felt certain I would catch sight of him – he surely couldn't be far away? His seal-dark hair, the mischief in his face and the feeling that I had seen him somewhere before, would make him instantly recognisable.

But I couldn't find him. Somehow he had slipped away; perhaps he had vanished into one of the bathing machines. I wandered a little further, hearing the shouts of the children and the punctual surge of the sea. Then, with reluctance, I turned back. Why did his face seem so familiar? I chased an elusive memory... Then suddenly I stood still. The woman, the tall dark woman who had also (but long ago) stood to look at me, as the boy had done, on the shore. Looked, but not spoken. He resembled her. I was aware of mystery, something unexplained. But perhaps of no account.

August 28th
This day began with its usual calm, but did not end so.

First, Alexander arrived, as usual without warning, in the early afternoon. He greeted the children, I thought with some abstraction, and when we were alone I was aware of a suppressed excitement. However, he said nothing except that he was glad to see me and that I was looking well. I thought then, as he turned aside, that his face fell into lines of anxiety, but perhaps this was merely fatigue from the journey.

It was after the evening meal, the children in bed, the house quiet, that he took me out into the dusky garden, where lamp-light fell a little way on to the grass. We sat on the wicker chairs and he lit a cigar. The scent mingled with the salt of the sea and the night plants. I waited in silence, looking towards a last streak of light above the sea. Then Alexander said, 'I have a surprise for you, my dear.'

His voice betrayed no kind of unease. On the other hand, it did, I thought, sound a little like a line he'd rehearsed. He went on. 'I'm taking you for a holiday. We're going to Italy.'

Indeed, at this time many English people took themselves to Italy, including Mr and Mrs Robert Browning – but Alexander and I had not travelled much abroad. He had been a few times to Paris on business, for some of his clients lived there, and some in Boulogne, but I had not gone with him. Indeed he had not suggested it. I said simply, 'Why?'

'Oh, my dear, does one have to have a reason for a holiday? I've been working very hard, and a client has recommended an hotel in Florence, not far from the Ponte Vecchio. Such a beautiful city! There was trouble there, of course, not so many years ago, but that splendid fellow, Giuseppe Garibaldi, restored the kingdom. He came here to the island to visit your poet at Farringford.'

Yes, I remembered that, amongst the shining names of those who had visited the house... But Florence now? How long would we stay? I asked. Alexander made a movement of his shoulder. 'I don't know. A few weeks. It is holiday time, after all.'

I was silent. Then I said, 'The children?'

'My dear, you spend hours and days with the children. It's time they learned that mothers and fathers have lives of their own.'

I said, 'If we are some weeks away, that will mean the end of the island for this summer.'

'Goodness! Do you not see enough of the island? *Every* summer? You must learn to love other places.'

He made my feeling for the island sound simple, even childish. I could think of no reason not to go with Alexander to Italy. But the air in the garden seemed suddenly to grow colder and soon I went back into the house. I went quietly into the children's rooms. Marigold was awake, reading; Sylvia, Rebecca and Toby were asleep. Children asleep have a profound innocence, I thought: they are open to all the winds of the world's harm and know nothing of it. I lingered for a few moments, watching them, then turned away to prepare myself for bed.

Alexander still sat on alone in the garden. When I looked from the window I could see the smoke of his cigar. He was not reading; simply sitting there. Then I put out the lamp.

September 5th – Florence

Yes, of course it is a beautiful city. Today Alexander and I took a carriage up to the Piazza Michelangelo and looked out over the rooftops. The sky was hyacinth blue, so that the rust colour of Brunelleschi's Dome, and the white of Giotto's tower were most beautifully defined, with the Tuscan hills beyond. Perhaps it was true, as Alexander had said, that I should learn to love other places.

Alexander himself was something of a puzzle to me. He seemed glad of my company and took pleasure in showing me the golden places of the city by day, then finding small secluded restaurants on the Lung'Arno, where we could watch the carriages pass by under the lamplight in the green-blue Italian dusk. The river ran gently, tamed, unlike the sea.

When, back at the hotel, we retired for the night, he would

make love to me in his usual fashion. There were, as ever, no words. Yet there were moments in the day when I caught in his manner or face something of melancholy, which was unlike him. These occasions were brief, and I daresay he thought I didn't notice them.

Letters came from Nanny, with news of the children. Letters from the children too. I read these with a feeling of longing, mixed with guilt, for I did truly love the Italian city, the harsh/sweet clang of the Angelus, the scent of incense in the churches, the Ghiberti doors. And I could not have stood and wondered at these with the children clamouring for attention and getting bored. But the letters, the sloping capitals, the rows of kisses... I showed them to Alexander, but he simply smiled and said, 'Charming; what nice children they are!' and clearly had no great interest.

The sunny days passed, with something of the monotony of a picture gallery which is showing works of an almost exactly similar kind. Yes, it was a beautiful place, but we could not linger here indefinitely. Surely we must soon return to London, when the children's governess would come daily to the house, and autumn life would begin? When I said as much to Alexander, he grew a little impatient. 'One doesn't come to Italy just to glance round and return home! One takes one's time, learns a little Italian ... enough to say *grazie* and *prego* and *buon' giorno* if nothing else.' A small note of contempt here, I spoke no Italian, only a little French, as taught by my governess. But I persisted that though I truly appreciated the city, I wanted to have some idea of when we would return to England. His face for a moment showed no expression at all, which I knew meant that he was annoyed but was not saying so.

And then the letter came.

September 25th

I write now, because it gives some ease. Not much, I do not think one can ask for much ease in this life, however pleasant it may sometimes be.

The letter we received in Italy came from Beatrice; I knew a moment of mistrust when I saw it. Beatrice wrote seldom and when she did it was to some purpose.

She had written to Alexander; he scanned the letter with his usual rapidity, then without a word handed it to me. Beatrice had written: 'I am not happy about Rebecca. Nanny tells me that her "throat" is a usual thing, but I am not convinced. She does not seem well to me. Dr Lang is reassuring, but then he always is.' (Beatrice had an abiding contempt for Dr Lang.) 'I would not write as I do if I did not feel that you should return. It's possible all will be well. In which case, I shall have alarmed you unnecessarily. But I should be doing less than my duty if I didn't tell you of my concern.'

I put the letter down with such dread in my heart that for a moment I couldn't speak. The breakfast room of the hotel become suddenly an evil place. With a dry throat I said, 'We must go back. At once.' Alexander looked at me in silence, but he made no disagreement. How could he? Beatrice had never shown more than superficial concern for the children. It was unlike her to sound alarms.

He said at last, 'You must go. I have to stay here longer.'

A feeling of outrage made me catch my breath. 'You mean you aren't coming? You'd let me go back alone?'

His face was brooding, removed from me. He said, 'It's better if I follow you. I'm sure all will be well.'

I had few words for him as I packed and prepared for the journey. I was so full of dread that I hadn't the energy to give way to wrath. The journey passed like a dark dream, towns, stations, other travellers, the cross-Channel steamer, the sea giving me no comfort. Only one thought, only one hope in my head: Rebecca. 'Oh, my darling,' I said, 'get well. Please get well. Wait for me. I'm coming back to you. Get well. Please God – if you exist – make her well.'

The long journey was nearly done. The beloved place, now a background to dread. The horse carriage took me to the house. I had one word in my head all the time – please, please, please. Beatrice opened the door, Nanny stood behind her. There seemed to be another figure, but I had no time for any of them. I went running upstairs.

The bedroom was shadowed. I went quickly to the bedside. Rebecca lay, drowsy, sweat on her face, hair damp. A man whom I did not know stood in the shadows of the room. I knelt by the bed. Rebecca looked at me, at first, I thought, puzzled. Then her lips moved. 'Mama?'

48

I said clearly with as little emphasis as I could, 'Yes, darling, I'm here. Now you're going to get well.' She smiled and closed her eyes. I was very frightened, but determined to show nothing. I became aware of the man on the other side of the bed. He was not very tall, but a good deal younger – and of greater authority – than Dr Lang. I looked at him with immense pleading, but he simply made a gesture to lead me from the room.

He told me that Rebecca's 'sore throat' had become septicaemia and that there was little he could do. Beatrice, he explained, had summoned him from Newport, but by the time he reached the house, it was too late.

I had some kind of defence: I refused to believe him. I went back to the bedside, took her hand which was damp and hot, and said, 'You'll get well, darling. Quite soon we'll go down to the shore again.' She murmured something that sounded like, 'Yes, Mama.'

I don't think she said more. She smiled at me once or twice, and I tried to give her a sip of water, but the liquid spilled. I stayed there by the bedside for a time that was neither long nor short; it was not ordinary time. The doctor was back in the room. Were Nanny and Beatrice there? I don't remember. Rebecca's eyes were closed. The fear rose and rose within me because I was losing hold on hope, and I didn't dare do that. I said a lot of words, I don't know if she heard them.

When there seemed to be some alteration in her breathing, he drew closer to the bed. I saw some huge menace coming towards me that I had no courage to face. I saw a quiet come on Rebecca's face, and heard a kind of sad sigh, then silence. There was nothing terrible. The young doctor leant over her, listened for a heartbeat, lifted her eyelid. But I did not need his glance of commiseration or the slight shake of his head. I knew. I had lost her. The agony had begun. Oh, my darling.

Chapter 5
Kate and Perdita – 1940

Kate laid the book aside. Grief is common country, she thought; something shared. Perhaps the loss of a child is the most painful, the last outpost. And that touches a nerve, just now.

She rose, poured herself a drink (where would the next bottle come from in these times of shortage?) and lit a cigarette. Sounds of the raid persisted sullenly as she paced the room, now in the small hours. Nearly three o'clock; Perdita was in bed. An echo of Isabel's grief, Kate thought, stayed in the room. And there was a little flow of ease in her own pain, as if across time she and Isabel touched hands, met in the country of the bereaved.

The story in the journals had become more than the revelation of past grief: it had a feverish quality, like a drug. As if I entered her dreams, she thought. There was that time when she saw danger and fire in the streets. Sixth sense, second sight – something of that kind. I get the feeling she's trying to tell me something. Isabel has gone, but those books are alive, not just words on a page.

An acceleration of sound from outside the room: the clang of a rescue lorry racing through the dark streets... I wish I'd told her about Charles, Kate thought. It was the true essence of loving – for me, at any rate. I think perhaps for him, too. More and more as time went on.

'We must tidy this up,' he had said once. 'I'm husband to no one as things stand. Laura and I live separate lives; you and I meet as if time were against us. It should be better than that.'

But time was against us, Kate reflected; totally against.

(And the words came to her mind again – 'You cannot conquer time.')

And now? Which problem to tackle first? The ATS? They'll come for me soon, she thought. Not tonight, it's too late, but perhaps tomorrow...

She turned, hearing the sound. Perdita barefoot in a dressing gown, face cleared of make-up, hair disarranged. Looking younger than ever, Kate thought. She came and sat by the fire. 'Couldn't sleep,' she said.

'The raid?'

'Perhaps. It's quiet up in Cumberland, of course. You been reading?'

'Yes,' Kate said, 'about Rebecca.'

Perdita hugged herself, giving a small shiver. 'Oh God, yes; the worst thing, surely? Yet she never talked of her.'

'We didn't ask,' Kate said. 'We didn't ask enough.'

'No, that's true. There's so much we don't know. Why was Grandmother so hard up when we knew her? Look at that life – nanny and cook and house in Russell Square or thereabouts ... not grand, perhaps, for those days, but not hard up, either.'

'There's more to read,' Kate said, 'if we've time.'

'Time?' Perdita asked.

Kate shrugged. 'Well – when all this is done, you have to get back to the children. And I – well, to say the least I have matters to sort out.'

She sat down in the chair opposite Perdita. For a few moments silence lay between them, with the danger outside. Then Perdita said, 'You're pregnant, aren't you?'

Kate looked at her glass. 'I believe so. How could you know?'

Perdita once more clasped her dressing gown about herself. 'Family,' she said. 'The old sixth sense – like Grandmother Isabel... What are you going to do?'

'God, I don't know.'

'Did you tell Charles?'

'No. There wasn't time. I thought there was going to be – I would have told him – but there wasn't. I haven't told anyone. There's a school of thought – to which I think I belong – that would say a 'termination' – I do hate the word 'abortion' don't you? – would be the best for everyone. If it can be achieved.'

'Is that what you want?'

'Oh God,' said Kate again, 'I don't know. I'm in a bloody awkward position. And – like most of the family – seriously short of cash. I've written nothing for a long time – not sure how it'll be when I try again...'

Perdita nodded, her face concentrated. 'Have you thought what Isabel would have said?'

Kate glanced at the shabby books. 'Oh – that world of children and Nanny and certainty —'

'Not all that certainty. There was Rebecca.'

'Oh, yes ... Rebecca.' Kate searched among the books and found the photograph. 'There she is – solemn, as if she knew what was coming.' That old grief came suddenly towards her, together with her own, and she drained her glass, blinked at the dying fire.

Perdita got up from her chair and put her arms round her. Kate, moved, reminded herself that Perdita had a husband away at war, and two children; subject, as they all were at this time, to danger and to change.

'Don't do anything yet,' Perdita said. 'Please don't. See what else she has to say.'

The words brought Kate to silence. She touched Perdita's hand. The drone of aircraft carried echoes of the sound of the sea.

Chapter 6
Isabel – 1885

September

The last of summer. The roughened seas, the emptying shore. I
have to stay here for a few more days. Alexander came at once,
but of course he didn't see Rebecca. My grief might have
turned to anger, save that I once caught sight of him sitting on
the edge of his bed in an attitude of such extreme despair that I
turned away. Certainly he was gentle with me. We buried her
on the island, in the quiet ancient cemetery with the lichened
stones (one dating back to 1645), the wide cypress tree and the
glimpse of the river Yar beyond. The church dates from before
the Norman Conquest, and these great distances of time gave
me a fraction of comfort.

I have tried to forgive Alexander for taking me away. He could
not have known. I have not asked him why he didn't return with
me. It doesn't seem to matter now. So many things don't matter
any more. I know I have to master this, if only for the sake of
Marigold and Sylvia and Toby, but it is a difficult task, something like, I imagine, recovery from a desperate illness.

Having this need for recovery in mind, I went one evening to
the rectory. The rector, who had taken the funeral, had said
that if I needed help at any time, he would be glad to do what
he could. I had taken these as the professional words that any
man of the church must utter in such circumstances. But something about the Reverend Piers Malleson made me pause – he
had shown such concern for us, had offered no pious platitudes
but seemed to enter our suffering, that it seemed to me that he
might indeed be able to give me the help which I so greatly
needed. Alexander made no objection, and I was glad that he

didn't offer to come with me, for I don't think that a conversation between the three of us would be of much relevance.

Piers Malleson received me in what appeared to be his study. I had not before been inside the house and only knew it from 'open days' in the garden. He motioned me to sit down and sat himself in the chair before his desk. He was a man of perhaps forty, but his hair was thickly grey, his expression calm, unsmiling, patient. He gave me no introductory words, did not enquire into my health or spirits, and this, while it well suited my mood, did not quell my anger.

'You are going to tell me,' I said, 'that all is well because Rebecca is with God.'

He seemed to look at this as if it were a new and surprising suggestion which had not so far occurred to him. Then he shook his head. 'Whatever those words mean, they will convey no comfort to you now.'

'Then what can you say to me?' I still spoke in anger, which he seemed to accept with accustomed patience.

Then he said, 'I can tell you some of the words that I would repeat to myself after my wife's death.'

For a moment I knew that entirely self-regarding resentment of those in pain confronted, as it were, with competition.

He went on, 'Psalm one hundred and three. One of my favourites. Do you know it?'

'I have read the psalms,' I said with some belligerence. 'I read them as poetry.'

'Which of course they are. There is a line – "He remembereth that we are but dust"—'

I interrupted him, still angry. 'But *does* he, Mr Malleson? *Does* he? I must say, I doubt it. I doubt it extremely.'

He was listening, it seemed to me, with absorbed attention, still patient. 'Yes,' he said at last, 'you have every right to doubt. I shouldn't really expect anything else at this time.'

Briefly, I was disconcerted. I looked round the shrouded study, lit only by an oil lamp. A masculine place, I thought, with books and papers placed haphazardly; pipe in the ashtray, ash scattered about. The room of a widower.

'You are in very harsh country,' he said. 'Bare, like a wilderness. And I can give you no escape from it: you have to go through...'

Perversely, I was angry because he had not offered me the kind of comfort which I could despise. 'And supposing I can't? Supposing I can't bear to live in the "wilderness", that I cannot bear to remember Rebecca, find her toys, her dresses, hear her voice calling for me.' I was releasing it all on him; I had not meant to be tearful, but I had to control my voice.

He looked at me with pity then. 'Have you thought –' he spoke carefully – 'that you are privileged?'

'Privileged!'

'Yes, you've a right to be angry. But you have encountered a depth of pain—'

'I have lost a *child*!' I stormed at him. 'A child I loved. The one I loved best of all.'

He sat still; only a small twitch at the side of his mouth showed that my words had touched him. 'I know. Perhaps I can't know the exact nature of your grief, because none of us truly knows another, as Sir Thomas Browne said. But I know you are in a place where there seems to be – ' he corrected himself ' – where there *is* no comfort. I can't, as I say, change that – much as I wish I could. I will just try to leave a few words with you that you may reject now, but later perhaps remember.'

I made some attempt to listen to him. I could see that he tried to speak the truth as he saw it; I could see also that despite his calm of manner he spoke under some strain. A strain which I caused him.

'You will have come through the darkest place. In time you will have more to give – the comfort that now I can't give you; you will have become someone of deeper compassion—'

'That's not what I want! I want Rebecca!'

He watched me in silence and said nothing obvious. In fact, nothing at all: the small lamp-lit room was silent except for the drift of sea wind outside. Again I felt that irrational anger because he didn't offer me the pious comfort that I could easily reject. It had after all been a foolish exercise to come here – he had nothing to give me. I couldn't blame him, for no one had anything to give me.

I rose to leave, but, rising too, he put out a hand and touched my arm. 'I've failed you, of course. But try to remember that my thoughts and prayers are with you. Those are not just words. Since Rebecca died I have thought constantly of you, offered my prayers. I believe you love poetry ... "More things are wrought by prayer than this world dreams of ..." Is that not what the poet said?'

I nodded briefly. The truth was, I perceived, that I did not want to be comforted. I gave him some words of thanks, which I knew in truth were inadequate. Indeed, as I turned to go, I wished I could have said more, for his efforts had been palpable.

He summoned a carriage for my brief journey back to Rosecroft. As I caught a glimpse of his face in farewell I saw that it was marked with lines of exhaustion. He stood in the doorway of the rectory with the light behind him.

The image stayed with me, uncomfortably, as I returned home.

September 30th

I had not expected to see Piers Malleson again before we left for London. I was much concerned with Marigold and Sylvia – Toby was too young to understand, though he looked about him with puzzled enquiry, as if searching for the absent sister. But Marigold and Sylvia were another matter. Marigold is ten years old and death is real to her. I mean that she is able to understand the idea of it – not that anyone can explain the mystery. Nanny has a simple answer: 'Little Rebecca has gone to be with the good Lord' – but that is not enough for Marigold. She has a lot of questions: but *how* has she, why has she? I cannot satisfy her. Nor can I meet that stab of jealousy which I know she feels because I grieve for Rebecca and her presence is not enough to comfort me.

Sylvia, nearly four years old, is in some ways the most greatly disturbed. She cries and has tantrums. (And she too is jealous: I know that.) I have tried to show her that I love her, knowing that she has been faced with a fact full of menace and beyond her understanding. But sometimes my patience runs out and I speak sharply, telling her to be quiet. I have an unhappy feeling that some sort of damage has been done to a nature which has always been wayward, a little unbalanced.

And Alexander? I have never known in truth how much he felt for the children – deeply felt, I mean, not just being proud of them when they were well behaved. But with Rebecca's death, something has changed in him. He doesn't talk about her – I would be glad of that – but he does not. He is a man whose mind is clouded with . . . anxiety? Fear? Simply sadness for loss? Perhaps he regrets our journey to Florence, for if we had been at home, would it not have been possible to have summoned medical help more quickly? I have not said anything like this to him – though I have thought it – for that would be too cruel. And there is something about Alexander at this time which prevents me from saying anything to him which might wound. He is very quiet with me, quite unlike himself. But I do not feel a complicity of grief – he is not entirely at one with me in mourning Rebecca. If our eyes meet, there is strangely, for a moment, no communication. I am also aware that within his undoubted grief there is a small shard of resentment at the idea of failure (if such it can be called): he has always cherished the idea that he and his family are successful – better-looking, more brilliant, more to be admired than others. He has never liked people to be sorry for him. And he sees death perhaps as the ultimate failure.

It was at about half past five on this day that the doorbell sounded. I thought at first it might be Beatrice, for though she had said her farewells, she might have some further words to say to us. Beatrice had been good to me – or at least, she had tried to be. Something, I thought – as with Alexander – held her back from true compassion; she could not put her arms round me. But her manner was gentle – once I even caught the glint of tears in her eyes when her glance happened to fall on some discarded toy of Rebecca's.

But it was not Beatrice at the door. Bessie showed the Reverend Piers Malleson into the living room. Alexander greeted him with, I thought, a degree of reserve: he never liked the unexpected. However, he invited him to sit down.

Piers Malleson refused a whisky and soda. He said, 'I was visiting close by and I wanted to see you both once more. I hope I don't come at an awkward time: the clergy can sometimes feel that they have the right of entry at any time of day, but of course that isn't true.'

Though he spoke with his usual calm, I felt oddly embarrassed for him, as if he were a relative or friend for whose presence I was responsible. Alexander made some suitable response, and he went on, 'I just wanted to say – to you both – I hope this tragedy won't keep you from the island.' He looked down at his hands. 'I think that is important. The island has been a haven. Especially to you, Mrs St Clair.' He gave a small smile in my direction. The smile pleased and disturbed me at the same time, for I thought it a little forced. 'The place has one dark memory for you, of course. But there are other memories too. Gentler ones, and those have their own importance. It would be sad – we should all be sad – if you decided not to return.'

Before I could speak, Alexander, standing before the mantelpiece, said, 'You will understand, Mr Malleson, that just at the moment it is impossible for my wife and myself to make any decisions. Our life has been overturned. There will be plenty of time to talk about these things when we are back in London.'

'Of course. I was only anxious that you should not be, let me say, moved by grief to decide too hastily.'

'I'm not in the habit, Mr Malleson, of making rapid decisions. Long years in the legal profession have cured me of that fault, if I ever had it.'

Piers Malleson acknowledged this thrust with a small downturn of his mouth, and I said quickly, 'But we *shall* come back. One day. I don't know yet how soon. I couldn't leave the island for ever.'

I saw the quick frown on Alexander's face. If Piers Malleson saw it, he gave no sign, but simply said, 'Well, I'm glad of that. Yes, very glad.'

He was not a man (even so early I know this) to show embarrassment, to make confused apologies. Nevertheless the conversation after that ran uneasily, and I felt a kind of relief when he rose to go. Our acquaintance had been so brief, and of course I could not be certain that I should ever see him again. For when I did return to the island (whenever that might be) he would perhaps have moved on somewhere else. But as he took my hand in farewell, I remembered his attempts to give me comfort and wished there was time to say that I was grateful to him, that I remembered his words. But there was no more time. He was out of the house, and Alexander closed the door with a sound that spoke of finality.

'Well now, my dear. We need not discuss that, I think. Our bags are packed. London, now.'

Chapter 7
Isabel – 1888

August

A steel-bright morning, perhaps too brilliant. The sea not blue, but a kind of burning silver. Even the cries of children as they kick the dazzling water seem muted by warmth.

Yes, I have at last returned to the island. It has been a strange home-coming. I approached it with a mixture of dread and excitement, almost as if I expected to find Rebecca there.

As the familiar house came in sight I felt a clutch at my heart, a mixture of pleasure and pain. There was one moment when I almost wanted to turn back, but Marigold, without any warning, put her arm through mine. She is thirteen now, and can show sudden bursts of affection. Sylvia nearly seven shows no outward emotion, but there is something in her silence that troubles me. Toby, nearing four, is simply excited at the idea of a holiday – he is the sunniest of the children, and makes me laugh. He doesn't remember Rebecca, and his joyful innocence comforts me. There is life beyond pain.

Nanny is still with us. She has a look of disapproval as we approach the bay. She, I know, is against our return, though she doesn't say so; she thinks we should bury the island with the past. If I let it, this would make me angry, for she seems to say that we are not giving due reverence to Rebecca's memory, which is profoundly untrue. Nanny is also distrustful of the condition of the house – in these years Rosecroft has been occupied by other tenants and she has no confidence that they will have left the place as she would have done.

Alexander is not with us. I can't deny that this is something of a relief. In London, after Rebecca's death, he would return

59

later and later from work, tired, abstracted, inclined to be irritable. Indeed, the house in Russell Square became less and less congenial to me; it would be almost true to say I was unhappy there. The house seemed to echo, as if when I entered a room a whispering suddenly ceased. It was if the place housed an enemy.

My dreams at that time were dark, bringing me suddenly awake. Memory of them was confused, but there seemed to be two dominant figures; the woman who all those years ago had looked so penetratingly at us all on the shore – the woman whose look had shown a kind of arrogant pity; and the boy, the dark boy, with his wet shining hair, who had resembled her, and had so impressed me that I had followed him, losing him in the crowd. They recurred most vividly and with unexplained menace.

Yes, I was glad to be away from the house and back on the island with the children. Beatrice showed a degree of high spirits on our arrival which I had not at all expected. The more because it was in such contrast to Alexander's mood in London. 'It's a good thing,' she said, 'that you've come back. One must lay ghosts.'

She did not speak unkindly; I thought she made an effort to be on good terms with me. I agreed as I watched the children. 'Yes,' I said; and added that it would be good if Alexander could lay them too. 'It seems to me,' I said, 'that he is not himself.'

For a moment Beatrice's face tightened and I thought she was going to rebuke me as she often did. But then she gave a quick not-quite-real smile and said, 'He's working very hard. And he's approaching middle-age. Over forty! We are none of us getting any younger.'

Beatrice, like her brother, I reflected, fell easily into cliché, but this was not the time to remark on that.

August 15th

All the same, her words recurred to me the next day. Here was the island once more, but though the rocks and the sea were blessedly familiar, I was aware of change. First it was said that the poet had been gravely ill with rheumatic fever – he was after all nearing eighty. I had so great a veneration for him that it was like hearing of the illness of a loved friend. He had not long ago written some lines that touched the raw nerve of my own loss:

> I climbed on all the cliffs of all the seas,
> And asked the waves that moan about the world
> Where? do ye make moaning for my child?

I often turned to *In Memoriam*, and as I did so thought of the old man who – as I did – had loved the island. 'Close to the ridge of a noble down' he had described his house, whose shape I knew so well; the place where he 'watched the twilight falling brown...' Twilight. Yes, he was an old man now, but old men, I thought, had mystery, being so near their end. He had written other lines:

> The silver year should cease to mourn and sigh
> Not long to wait
> So close are we, dear Mary, you and I
> To that dim gate.

The words 'dim gate' sent a small shiver down my spine: I was too near the heyday of my own life to give much thought to death, yet somewhere at the heart of all those things I loved – the sea and the tall cliffs and the cropped grass of the Down – lurked the knowledge of that gate: nothing could dispel it.

Then there was the Queen at Osborne House. Rumour had it that her strength was failing – that long reign drawing to its end. Change, I thought (as many have no doubt thought before me), how gradually – but how devastatingly – it slips through life. Summers into autumn, with those inevitable leaves 'that strew the brooks in Valombrosa'. How I had loved that line. And change must have events in store that I could know nothing of, and for a moment I was afraid.

It was later in this day that I took the children for a walk over the Down. Nanny did not come with us; she had a heavy cold and I told her to rest in bed. Indeed, I was glad to be alone with the children. Toby trudged with a kind of masterful determination. In fact, it is Toby who cheers me most: he is such a lively – even comical child, clowning and making jokes

– already he seems to look on the world as a miraculous absurdity. (Perhaps it is.) Sylvia, I think, is a little jealous of him, but Marigold is old enough to transcend this, and she is charming with him, at her best. She takes time to play with him and laugh at his (very simple) jokes. She is already something of a beauty in her long skirt, and with her long copper hair. On this day on the Down she walked with a lazy stride, as if she knew that she looked graceful there. Only Sylvia struck a contrary note: she complained that walking made her tired and she didn't laugh when Toby did a comic dance, flapping his arms and spinning till he fell over. Sylvia too was a pretty child, her hair a more brilliant red than Marigold's, but her prettiness was often marred by a look of discontent. This could suddenly vanish and she would fling herself into my arms with wild affection.

I walked more slowly than they did, on the ridge of the Down with the sea far below, watching them with content – which was suddenly broken by a call from Marigold.

'*Mama*! Mama, come quickly. Sylvia's gone too near the edge and says she can't move!'

I went rapidly over the short turf. Sylvia had wandered close to the edge of the cliff and now sat crouched on the sloping path in a kind of terror, with her back to the sea. She shivered away from Marigold's encouraging hand and paid no attention to Toby who kept saying, 'It's all right, Syl! It's all right! You won't fall into the sea and go splash! No, you won't.' She was not in real danger, I could see that, but she had frightened herself into thinking she was.

I had to quiet a moment of panic: she would catch that immediately. I said calmly, holding out my hand, 'Just come towards me, darling. You'll be quite safe.'

She stayed as she was, head down. 'I can't. I can't. I'll fall. I know I will.'

'*Will* she?' Toby asked, with a mixture of anxiety and relish.

I said, 'No, of course not. She's quite safe.'

'I'm not! I'm not!' Sylvia cried, and there flashed through my mind the idea that Sylvia would never be safe.

It was at that moment that I heard the voice behind me. 'D'you need help?'

I turned to see the Reverend Piers Malleson. He stood there, wind ruffling his hair, and smiled at me. He wore a Norfolk jacket and flannels, and might – except for his collar – have been any man out for a walk on the Down.

Though it was a long time since I had seen him, he seemed greatly familiar, his face not much changed. Perhaps there was even more grey in his hair, but the eyes were bright and calm as I remembered them. I told him what the trouble was, and he said, 'Well, I think we can do something about that.'

'Oh, good, good,' said Toby.

Piers Malleson held out his stick with the handle towards Sylvia. 'Now, young lady,' he said, 'if you just catch hold of that, hold it firmly, you'll be perfectly all right. Put out your hand – your right hand – and take hold ... no, don't be afraid. There's nothing to be afraid of.'

Perhaps the power of a masculine voice cancelled her fear and moved her to action. Cautiously she put out one hand as he'd instructed her, and slowly, trembling a little, got to her feet and moved forward into safety.

'Oh, hooray!' Toby said. 'Now you won't go splash.'

I comforted Sylvia and wiped her tears. Marigold played the elder sister, but with a touch of scorn. 'You were a silly ass to get in such a state.' However, she stroked Sylvia's hair and took her hand.

With Toby prancing and shouting 'Hooray!' every now and again, the children went ahead. Piers Malleson and I walked together. I was beginning to recall that we had not met for a long time, and on that occasion I had been angry and ragged with grief. Yet, though so much time had elapsed, I had a sensation of familiarity, as if we had only recently broken off a conversation of some interest, if not intimacy. We talked of the poet at Farringford, and of his health. Piers Malleson told me that he had visited him.

'You went to *see* him?' I said.

He smiled and said yes, he had been invited. He had gone in some trepidation, for Alfred Lord Tennyson was known to have a rough way with strangers – especially, perhaps, men of the cloth. But the great man had, Piers Malleson said, been in expansive mood, helped maybe by many glasses of port.

'You really spoke to him?' I said. 'I dreamed I did once.'

He smiled as we walked on. 'I spoke of *In Memoriam*, of

course. But also of his son, Lionel, who died of fever on his way home from India.' He paused then and glanced at me, but I made no reference to Rebecca. Not then. He went on, 'We talked of Mr Browning, whom he admired – he is generous to other poets. We spoke of his poem, '"Bishop Bloughram's Apology" – I expect you know it – where he talks of "the grand Perhaps"?' I did know it, but was surprised that he should assume so. 'You may wonder,' he said, 'why he should have invited me – an obscure rector – to his house?'

I walked on briefly in silence, then said with a smile, 'No, that thought had not occurred to me.'

'Ah! Well – some little while ago I gave a sermon on doubt. You'll remember the line in his poem: "There lives more faith in honest doubt, believe me than in half the creeds"? I preached on this with some force – and I hope not too much length. Quite a number of the congregation objected. Others – a minority – were grateful. The small event had surprising repercussions, which came to the ears of the poet. So ... I received the royal command.'

I watched the children as they ran ahead. 'Doubt ...' I said.

'You may remember ... we spoke some time ago, after Rebecca's death.'

There was a little change between us. I felt the wind from the sea, as if it had for the first time touched my skin. He went on, 'I quoted the psalm: "He remembereth that we are dust". And you questioned that. I remember it very well. Your exact voice as you questioned it.'

I was silent. I too remembered; I could see his room, dusk-shadowed, his figure opposite me. I could remember that raw grief, now softened, never entirely healed. As it would never entirely heal.

Piers Malleson went on, head down, as he strode over the turf, 'I must confess, I've never forgotten that. It has stayed in my mind all this time.'

Yes, the day had changed. Glancing at him I could see now that the years had made their mark, more than I had at first supposed. I could see that he was a troubled man. We went on in silence for a while, and the children's voices came to me, lively, part of a different day. Briefly, I envied their innocence, their freedom from the demands of adulthood.

Piers Malleson said, 'I would like to call on you one evening. Just to talk a little further. Or perhaps you'd find that unwelcome at the end of the day?'

The children had stopped there ahead of us. Toby was turning somersaults on the grass. 'No,' I said, 'I wouldn't find it unwelcome.'

August 20th

The days seem to darken earlier and the sea comes in with greater strength – I can see the spray lifting against the rocks as if to give warning of fiercer winds to come.

This day is coloured by the memory of last evening.

As he had promised. Piers Malleson came to visit me. He came on foot and brought into the house traces of the evening air. He accepted brandy and sat in the chair opposite me – Alexander's chair.

I told him how much I had missed the island, and how glad I was – despite some shafts of sorrow – to be here again. He listened, hands clasped between his knees. Through the open window came the wash of the sea – it has a different sound at evening, like a farewell. He spoke easily enough – of the changes on the island, the new houses, the influx of visitors, since the Queen had, so to speak, put the place on the map by her long stay at Osborne. And, plagued by such visitors, the poet had moved with his family to the mainland, for the summer.

We returned to the question of doubt. It became clear to me that he had read widely of the poets – of Mr Browning and Mr Matthew Arnold in particular. He spoke of 'Dover Beach', of the withdrawing sea of faith. ' "Where ignorant armies clash by night," ' he quoted and went on, 'Sometimes I wonder ... we live in peace, but sometimes I feel the nearness of armies—'

He broke off as I gave a small exclamation. Hesitating at first, I told him of my dreams – dreams of threatened streets, full of light and danger, and the girl who walked beside me – the girl I knew and did not know ... I broke off. 'You will laugh at me, Mr Malleson. Or think I am a little mad.'

He never laughed at mystery, he said, and he seldom thought people mad unless they were in the last stages of lunacy. He smiled as he said this and I saw how the smile greatly lightened his face; the sombre lines vanished and he became a different man.

From then on the talk flowed more freely. (Perhaps dangerously freely?) He talked of the difficult country, you might say the wilderness, in which he now found himself. He could only speak the truth as he understood it, but the truth was summed up in those words 'honest doubt'. He had to counsel the young, marry the lovers, bury the dead and comfort the bereaved. 'I have to do all these things,' he said, 'with a great sense of uncertainty, of failure even. For after all, what is my purpose, if not to give assurance? And if I cannot do that, I had better leave this place and my calling. One can't live a pretence.'

He smiled again, though this time with some sadness. 'I mustn't burden you. But these are difficult times for belief.'

Perhaps, I suggested, all times were difficult for belief? He smiled again. 'Yes, indeed. But now... Not so long ago they buried Charles Darwin in Westminster Abbey. Rather strange, perhaps, for he has surely done more than any man in recent years to shake the solid structure of simple faith.'

I thought about this, and then said, 'I don't really see how any faith can be truly simple. For surely the whole matter is so vast and mysterious. Rebecca is gone into some place of which I have no knowledge ... not even a belief. And even you and I – ' a quick upward glance which I could not – or did not want – to read – 'even you and I, sitting here, will one day die, go into that mystery. My own children – God willing – one day will be old. They will perhaps have children whose future I shan't live to see. And they too will die. What are we – what is anyone – to make of it all?'

He smiled again. 'You said, "God willing"'

'It's a phrase,' I said, 'a word for fate.'

'Fate ... yes. Rather a bleak word, perhaps. We were talking of Mr Matthew Arnold. You remember the lines "... neither joy, nor love, nor light, Nor certitude, nor peace, nor help for pain".'

Yes, indeed, I said, and remembered that I had thought of them as I watched Toby by the shore.

He stayed a little longer and the talk was companionable, touching on true things which talk so seldom does. When he had gone I took down Mr Arnold's poems, and read of the

'Sea of Faith ... retreating to the breath of the night wind, down the vast edges drear, and naked shingles of the world.'
And then I read,

'Ah love, let us be true to one another
For the world which seems to lie before us like a land of
   dreams
So various, so beautiful, so new,
Hath really neither joy nor love nor light
Nor certitude, nor peace, nor help for pain.'

I shut the book, with the sudden shock going through me. I told myself to ignore it, for it was absurd. We were strangers.

But the conviction would not go away. There had been love and desire there in the room this evening.

I put the book back on the shelf and tried to put all other thoughts away with it.

Chapter 8
Kate and Perdita – 1940

Waking to daylight, Isabel's journal open on her beside table, Kate rubbed her eyes, sandy with long reading and short sleep. 'Love,' she muttered to herself. 'We might have known.'

She pulled on her dressing gown and drew the black-out curtains from the window. Morning showed the dust-clouded street, the aftermath of the raid. Someone somewhere was sweeping up broken glass, and an air-raid warden in tin hat, gas-mask slung over his shoulder, walked slowly, for the moment unoccupied.

She glanced again at the journal. Yes, Isabel, securely married to Alexander, with her three children, her doubts and her grief, loved and was loved by the nice reverend. That much was clear. The faded handwriting glowed with vanished but powerful life.

Breakfast, she told herself, for it was important to come to terms with the day. When she had found the meagre butter ration and a near-empty jar of marmalade she was joined by Perdita, also in a dressing gown, also tousled with sleep. She looked, as ever, just out of school. As Kate told her the story of Isabel's love, she listened with rapt attention. 'What came of it, d'you think?' she asked. 'For they didn't run off together – did they?'

Kate shook her head. 'I remember Isabel at Grandfather's funeral – just. She was old then. No, there was no running away.'

'I'd like to think,' Perdita said, 'that sometime they were happy. In spite of everything. I just would.'

'Maybe they went to bed together,' Kate said, grasping her

coffee mug. 'The Victorians did, you know, in spite of all those clothes. Even the clergy ... I wish I'd known. She'd have understood about Charles. Why do people keep so many secrets?'

'We're afraid to be known,' Perdita said.

'Oh, God, that's true.'

A small silence across the breakfast table as they faced each other, Kate alive to Perdita's enquiring sympathy. She said at last, 'You don't have to worry about me. I've fallen into an awful lot of holes, but I've always managed to dig myself out.'

Perdita acknowledged this, as if from long experience. 'All the same,' she said, 'now must be different.'

'Not an easy one, I'll admit,' said Kate.

'If I could help? I would, you know.'

'Bless you, I know you would. But this is my particular hurdle. A small one, I suppose you'd say, in the midst of war. Grandmother talked of "Mr Browning" – there's a line of his: "Perhaps the world will end tonight". I think that's how I'm looking at it. Perhaps it'll all be solved—'

The sound of the telephone cut her short. A precise female voice greeted her at some distance and asked for Perdita.

When Perdita came away from the telephone she said that her son, Danny, wasn't well: high temperature and a cough. 'Bronwen says I should go back. And I must. Because—'

'You think he's really ill?'

'No – I'm not frightened. Danny has a way of sending his temperature up at will, and bringing it down as fast. I think this is Bronwen's way of telling me that my place is with the children, and not with you in London. But I have to be sure.'

Rebecca's name, Kate thought, is unspoken between us. She said, 'Of course you must go. But I shall miss you.'

Risen from the table, Perdita tightened the cord of her dressing gown and said, 'I'll be back. As soon as he's better. I want to come with you to the island. For the ceremony – or whatever you call it – of the ashes. They keep asking you "Is Your Journey Really Necessary?" Well, yes; in this case it is. I shall be back.'

Kate went with Perdita to the station. The streets were shabby, here and there cordoned off; by contrast men and women were going about their business as if there was nothing amiss. There was a light but steady rain. There was no need, Perdita said, for Kate to come with her, but Kate said yes, there was, because she didn't want to lose Perdita before she must, nor did she want her to spend hours alone at the station because of bomb damage on the line, which there could easily be.

When they came to the station, they met the usual wartime confusion. The morning was cold, the floor grubbily wet. Soldiers and airmen stood about, with their packs beside them. The departure board showed 'Delays, due to enemy action'. Perdita's train, however, promised to leave on time. 'I suppose that's lucky,' Perdita said, 'you always have to allow for good luck, in spite of everything.'

Kate lingered by the crowded train, with Perdita safely inside. Farewells, kisses, the slam of doors: a place of parting. Perdita leaned from the carriage window, grasped Kate's hand, and said, 'Promise me you'll do nothing till I come back? Promise, Kate?'

Kate tried to say something in reply, but already there was the scream of a train's whistle, voices calling 'Goodbye!' and Perdita was being pulled out of sight into a distance of time and place.

'The flood has borne me far,' thought Kate, with a salute to Isabel. The empty rails gleamed as the train slid on its journey, and there was nothing to do in this place of departure but to walk away, hands in her pockets, huddled against the cold.

She had said goodbye in just such a place, in just such a way, to Charles. Waved, said I love you, please take care. Flung the useless words to him, seen the grin on his face, just heard him say, 'Be happy, darling,' before the train had drawn out, taking him away for ever.

Silly to cry, walking away from the noisy, wartime station. Simply Perdita returning to her children; simply that memory of Charles, *Be happy darling*; the large, still unanswered question that she carried with her; the sense of walking alone amongst many strangers.

Alone, except for Isabel.

Chapter 9
Isabel – 1892

September

The day is blowy, with intermittent sunshine. Autumn now; the visitors are fewer, though there are some who brave the colder sea. (Courage seems to me the most necessary attribute – after all, what else does one need?)

I have so much to write of that I scarcely know where to begin.

With what is nearest my heart? The children, of course. Toby with his clowning, his jokes and his friendliness: he is at home with everyone – the fisherboy on the shore, and even his Aunt Beatrice. This surprises me, but I can see that in spite of herself, she is beguiled by him. If she is going out of the room, he opens the door and bows deeply, but there is no mockery in it – or at any rate, not enough for Beatrice to perceive. He cannot of course remember Rebecca, though he has seen her photograph. 'Oh, poor Rebecca,' he said once. 'I don't suppose it was much fun to die. I don't think death is a nice word: why can't they call it something else?' Later he said, 'Couldn't someone think of a way to stop it?'

And the girls. Marigold – now at seventeen, her charm and gracefulness increased. A charm that sometimes abruptly fades when she doesn't get her way. Naturally enough she loves pretty clothes, and money is, I think, an abstract concept: the words 'it's too expensive' have no meaning for her; if she wants it, she must have it. She welcomes the glances of the young men – well, she is seventeen and pretty, what else can occupy her mind? Oh yes, I loved her, and hoped she would marry a man who would be strong enough to say no.

71

And Sylvia? As she grew older, my anxiety for her increased. Despite her marked talent for drawing (her governess, not an effusive woman, praised her work in strong terms), her nature was wild, swinging from excitement to anger, then a kind of melancholy. The anger troubled me most, for I could see how much, when it was over, it distressed her. Then she was lost, wanting, yet not able, to show sorrow or regret. My heart aches for her.

Nearest to my heart. Yes, the children, of course.

But there is this other love.

How am I to write of it? I have never had much time for romantic stories; the words with which people speak of 'love' often seem to me exaggerated, even wearisome. Yet if I tell the truth I must say that my love for Piers Malleson is deep, even savage, something that came to me with total shock, a sensation new to me. I had not felt this for Alexander. I had believed I loved him, but I knew now that this was not so.

This was love. I was not a young woman – I had a daughter of seventeen, I had shared my marriage bed with Alexander and I was not aware of any bodily hunger. Life was as full and comfortable as any woman had a right to expect. I had the abiding loss of Rebecca – not a day passed when I didn't think of her. I had too a growing concern about Alexander – at times I even wondered if he was ill. But if I made any such enquiry, he brushed it – as usual – almost angrily aside. And indeed at other times he seemed in perfect health and spirits. I had much to make me content.

But I was aware of this powerful sensation, the quickened beating of my heart if I heard mention of Piers' name; the deep pleasure I had in his company, in our talks together which ran as easily as mountain water, our voices tripping over each other in harmony or argument.

I was for the present content with such limits to our meetings. I was not so simple that I did not see danger in the close companionship of a widower and a married woman whose husband was often absent.

Perhaps I gave too much weight to the idea that a man of the cloth is in some way different from others. I couldn't deny that he enjoyed my company – no, more than enjoyed it. One evening as he rose to say good-bye he put his hand on my arm, and the small contact almost made me catch my breath. But that was all. He dropped his hand and bowed briefly, and left me. Standing there I heard the sound of wheels, the jingle of harness, the horse's hooves. I had a sensation of loss which I told myself was absurd. But it persisted, though I took my sewing and held it close to the oil lamp. All the time I could hear the sea, the night sea, and some of the poet's words recurred to me about the sea on the cold grey stones and 'the thoughts that arise in me'.

September 13th

And news today that the poet is very ill. In fact, near his end. First the Queen's failing health and now this. I am suddenly afraid of the relentless passing of time; nothing is proof against it, nothing at all.

When Piers came to see me last evening I tried to tell him something of my fear. My words sounded naive, even to myself, for what is there new in the passing of time, the fear which we all have of death? But I spoke vehemently, and it occurs to me that the root of my vehemence lay not only in my fears for my children, but in this unspoken love. I would soon have to return to London, and Piers had spoken freely about his uncertainty, the question of leaving the Church, possibly the island; it seemed likely that I might never see him again. I spoke passionately, though without any word of love. But the air in the room was changed, this I was aware of —.

It was then that I heard the doorbell. I was not at all prepared for it and turned, surprised, waiting. Alexander? But Alexander would have a key, and though his arrivals were often unannounced, he never came so late. Bessie, the parlourmaid, opened the door. 'Mrs Courtney, ma'am.'

I was certainly not prepared for Beatrice. And she, it was immediately clear, was not prepared for Piers Malleson.

She stood still, while Bessie quietly closed the door, and I wondered if the atmosphere in the room was as palpable to her as it was to me. Piers had risen to his feet, and of the three of us seemed the most composed.

Beatrice recovered herself. 'Why, Mr Malleson! I didn't expect to see you. You seem out of place.'

Piers gave an amused smile. 'I do hope not, Mrs Courtney.'

73

As Beatrice accepted a glass of Madeira wine and sat down, I doubted that I matched their composure. I was breathless and the sensation of time passing still held me. As I handed Beatrice her glass I saw that my hand trembled and knew that she wouldn't fail to notice that.

She spoke of Church matters with a note in her voice which suggested that these things concerned her and Piers, and left me aside. This was true, but I was not enjoying it. After a little while of these exchanges, she turned to me. I could see myself as I must appear to her, somewhat dishevelled, too bright of eye. She said, 'I have news of Alexander, my dear.'

'*You* have news—'

'He has not been well.'

'Not *well*? But ...'

Beatrice looked at me with a sudden glance which was familiar. 'He didn't want to worry you. He has been confined to bed with a slight fever, but he's better now.'

'I should have been told!'

I saw Piers glance at me, and Beatrice's eyes close in a moment's reproof. 'He was particularly anxious that you should not be worried. He is well now, and will be coming to the island to complete his recovery.'

I stopped myself from saying that I should have been told this also. In truth I knew in that moment that I didn't want Alexander to come to the island. Abashed, guilty, I sat silent while Beatrice resumed her talk of Church matters with Piers.

When she said she must go, he did also. I could see that he could do nothing else, yet I was angry, as a child is angry when his day does not go according to plan. (Perhaps all love, I thought, has an element of childishness in it.) Piers said that his pony and trap were tethered close by and he would gladly take Beatrice to her door.

There was nothing I could reasonably say or do. I followed them into the hall and through the open front door. I could smell the night air and hear the distant sound of the sea. As Beatrice went ahead of him, Piers turned to look at me and a faint smile showed on his face, as if he recognised my unspoken anger and would have eased it if he could. Indeed, he put out one hand to touch my arm. But at that moment Beatrice

74

turned also to glance over her shoulder, and a small look of triumph showed on her face.

September 15th
Early mist gave way to sun; the sea had the lazy movement of autumn calm.

Alexander was due at midday. I went to Orchards and chose the kind of food which I thought he would enjoy. (Perhaps an attempt to absolve myself from guilt.) This done, I walked up the road towards the poet's house. The drive which led to the house was quiet and spoke of absence. Some of the words I loved seemed to drift on the air: 'Man comes and tills the field and lies beneath, And after many a summer dies the swan.' Yes, one more summer was slipping away, and I was passionately concerned with the passing of time and the loss of love.

I walked slowly back towards Rosecroft, my basket on my arm. My skirt, the colour of hyacinth, swung from light to shadow as I walked. I don't know why I was at that moment aware of my appearance; it seemed that though the fashion I was wearing was entirely natural to me, it would one day seem extraordinary, even absurd. I perceived again at some depth of the imagination the girl whose presence so often haunted me – what sort of dress would she wear? I had the impression of some kind of uniform, but that didn't seem to make sense—

'Isabel.'

The voice came sharply into my wandering thought. I turned to see Piers Malleson at my side. I had not heard his step.

We faced each other there in the quiet sunny sea road. I didn't think he had before used my Christian name. He said, 'I shall not leave the island.'

The bald statement did not seem out of place. It was as if we had taken up a conversation only briefly interrupted. He went on, as I did not speak, 'Not yet,'

I stood still, seeing and not seeing the flow of my skirt into sunlight. 'Alexander is coming today.'

'Yes, so I understand.'

'Soon after that we shall have to return to London.'

We had begun to walk on together. After a little silence he said, 'But I shall see you next summer?'

I saw the long distances of autumn, winter, spring. I said,

'Yes ... if you stay here on the island. But will you stay in the Church?'

'For as long as I'm accepted by my bishop. I shall say what I believe – no more. I shall talk as we have talked – fully and openly. You've given me a great deal, my dear; taught me so much.'

'*I* have taught you?'

'Oh, yes.' He smiled, the ironic smile I had come to know. 'Perhaps by listening; perhaps that's how women always teach men. How most of us learn. I shall speak to the men and women in the pews as I've spoken to you. Then we shall see what will happen. Where I stand in the Church, inside or out.'

We paused again. Everything was being given to me, and everything taken away. Those few words of admission were as powerful as any declaration of love. We were in love and we had no hope. Standing there I tried to read his face and, as if I had asked him a question he smiled and touched my hand. It was a firm touch, and I stood upright to prevent myself from putting my arms round him, there in the sunlit road in view of any who might pass by. As if he knew this he gave me a look in which pity was mixed with love. I need help, I thought, but I didn't say it aloud.

When we parted, I walked the last steps to Rosecroft, lost in a cloud of speculation and fear. When the house came in view I stood still and drew my breath. There were the children, I reminded myself, there was Nanny (dear heavens, what would *she* say?), there were the preparations for Alexander's return. As I walked up the path Toby left his bat and ball and came running towards me. 'There is Mama,' he said. 'The beautiful Mama with a basket. I will carry it for you; I am a knight errant. What does 'errant' mean? I am Tobias, the knight errant. I carry baskets.' I bent down and hugged him. 'Oh,' he said, 'that was a noble hug. Fit for a knight ... Mama? Are you *crying*?'

'No,' I said, 'no ...'

'Can't possibly,' Toby said, 'be any reason to cry. At least, I don't think so. Unless perhaps you don't love us any more? *Any* of us? But we're really quite nice – at least, sometimes.'

'Oh, no,' I said, hugging him again. 'I love you all. I love you very much. Come along. Papa is coming this afternoon, and we must get ready for him.'

Toby released himself and strode off, making his hands into the shape of a trumpet and calling out, 'Papa is coming, Papa is coming, and we must get ready *soon*!'

I watched him, wiping my face, then went into the house. Sylvia was painting in the front room and Marigold was reading a love story. The house was the same, the children were the same – but I was changed.

September 16th

Alexander is here. I have greeted him, I hope, with an adequate welcome. I have, I trust, betrayed nothing. But this morning, before he was awake, I walked alone down to the shore. Oh, how glad I am of the sea! There was scarcely anyone about – a lone fisherboy and a man who walked with a dog. The tide was low; morning light made luminous the frill of surf on the shore.

Rebecca? Oh yes, the quiet of such a morning seemed to hold the echo of her voice; the pang went through me as it sometimes did with full force, and I said aloud, 'Oh, my darling.' I recalled that evening in Piers' room when I had spoken so passionately of my grief.

Oh, my darling.

Yes, the words were for Rebecca; but they were for him also. I could see him, sitting opposite me, listening to my grief. I stood there, looking out at the quietly moving sea. This was not the pain of loss, but it was pain. Of no great importance, I was aware of that. The wide sea, the tall and ancient cliffs, made it clear that the love of a married woman in her middle years for a man who was not her husband was of small significance. Yet I was made of love, like a girl, obsessed with longing. And this was new discovery; it became even clearer to me, as I turned to walk away from the shore, that I had never truly loved Alexander. I shivered a little at this knowledge, for it was not welcome. He was the father of my children – of all my children, including my lost Rebecca. I had lived with him – despite varying absences – for nearly twenty years.

I glanced about me as I sought for help, for I felt greatly troubled. I had known the depths of grief on Rebecca's death, I had known times of strain with Alexander – but I had, it seemed, till now, followed a more or less ordered path. (This

77

gave me no virtue; I had been fortunate in the pattern of my life, that was all.) But now I felt as if I had lost my way in difficult country, bewildered and without directions. And I thought yes, though I have not known this before, I have known it in my dreams: that fear-laden search for a place which I cannot find, the way growing darker and more full of menace.

As I came near to the house, I suddenly stood still. Ahead of me, further up the road, I saw Alexander talking with a young man. Alexander had his back to me, but even so I was aware of some stiffness in his stance, as if this were an encounter for which he was unprepared. The young man, as far as I could tell from this distance, appeared at ease. He wore an open shirt and a Norfolk jacket – a visitor on holiday, I presumed.

As I drew nearer, Alexander turned. Having had him so recently – and unhappily – in my thoughts, I felt a small shock in facing him. His expression showed nothing; then he gave a brief smile and said, 'My dear, this is a young friend from London, Jasper Vye.'

I looked for the first time fully at Jasper Vye. He was tall – almost as tall as Alexander, though perhaps not yet twenty. His hair was dark, his face nearly handsome, with perhaps too prominent a nose. But his eyes were large, dark and alight, it seemed with friendliness ... something else as well? I could not be sure.

He bowed and took my hand. While we exchanged the commonplaces of those who have just been introduced, I tried to focus on a thought that was dodging about at the back of my mind. Had I seen a picture of him somewhere? I asked him if he knew the island well, and he smiled, looking away, as if he judged his answer. Then he said, 'Oh, I used to know it very well. As a child. But this is my first visit for a long time.'

'Are you coming to see us, Mr Vye?' I asked, and again I saw hesitation in his face. But before he could answer Alexander said, 'I'm afraid Mr Vye has no time, my dear; he is returning to London tomorrow – isn't that so, Jasper?'

The young man gave a small inclination of his head, as if in obedience. Yes, he said, to his regret he had to return to London – he would take the morning ferry. Perhaps another time...

As Alexander and I walked back towards the house, I was

conscious of unease. 'Jasper Vye,' I said. 'You seem to know him well: you called him Jasper. But I don't know anything about him.'

Alexander said he was a young man whom he'd met in the course of his legal work. Friends on the island had invited him for a short stay.

'Jasper Vye,' I said. 'It's an unusual name.'

'Most names are unusual when you hear them for the first time.'

'Yes,' I said, 'but ...'

'But what?'

'His face puzzled me.'

Alexander gave a slight laugh and smoothed his hair against the breeze. 'Really? I wonder why? He's a perfectly ordinary young man.'

I did not think so, but I was silent, not being able to explain myself. Then, as the day progressed and the children claimed my attention, I forgot about Jasper Vye. Or nearly forgot.

After dinner, Alexander and I sat together, I with my sewing and he with the *Times* on his lap. The oil lamp enclosed us in a small pool of light. I saw that Alexander's eyes were closing and the paper slipping from his grasp.

I leaned forward. 'Alexander! It's too early to sleep.'

He grunted and sat upright. 'Not really asleep,' he said, as I have found everyone does if you accuse them of dropping off in a chair.

'All the same,' I said, 'Beatrice told me you'd been ill—'

'A slight fever – nothing more.'

'But why wasn't I told?'

He shrugged. 'Not worth bothering about.'

'But worth bothering Beatrice?'

He looked at me then as if I had offered him some food which he had no taste for. 'She was in town. Naturally she knew. It's of no importance; I'm quite well now.' He folded his paper. 'Toby is growing into a splendid boy. Such spirit!'

I agreed, accepting the change of subject, that Toby was a splendid boy. The words brought back to me that moment this morning, when he had greeted me, and I had felt my heart to be torn. I glanced across at Alexander, because Piers had come so forcefully into my mind that I felt that he must pick up the thought from the air. But then I reminded myself that it was not Alexander's fashion to 'pick things from the air'; the air about him contained his own thoughts and no others.

As we went upstairs Alexander said that though he was quite well, he would sleep in the spare room as he was inclined to be restless. I was unprepared for the tide of relief which swept over me. So, I thought, this is how it is going to be.

It was as I undressed, looking back over the day, that I recalled the young man, Jasper Vye. As is the way, when you are not searching for a fact, the answer suddenly came to me, the likeness which had puzzled me. 'The boy!' I said, aloud, there before the looking glass, unpinning my hair, my hands suddenly still. All those years ago, the boy with wet dark hair, whose presence had disturbed me on the shore, for whom I had searched, but lost in the crowd. Jasper Vye was so like him!

I stood there, pins in my hand, seeing and not seeing my reflection in the glass... Perhaps it was an absurd fancy: after all, that had been a child, this was a young man. One could have no certainty. But as I prepared myself for bed, the memory returned the two faces seemed to merge into one, and that night I dreamed I was searching for the young man as I had searched for the boy at the edge of the shore.

Chapter 10
Isabel – 1894

July

There is no wind today. But this doesn't bring calm, for the air is stifling, the sea shining with a brassy light.

I cannot be sure how long I shall stay on the island. So much has happened, so much has changed. That is why I need to write again.

The small changes first. They have built new houses where before there were open fields: villas, obtruding like strangers in a familiar room. Many more visitors come to the island now, and quite often one sees young women on bicycles, which I find rather charming. Indeed, I have one myself now, though I could not call myself young any more.

The poet has gone. He died at his house on the mainland. They buried him in the Abbey as they had buried Mr Browning three years before – the Dean, I understand had asked Lord Tennyson if Mr Browning should be buried in the Abbey, and the poet had said, 'Of course.' Members of the Tennyson family, I believe, still occupy the house, the stately Farringford, but it is not the same. Sometimes I walk over the Down and follow the path that leads towards the house. I can see its familiar shape, but I am aware of a presence gone. The words of his poems echo in my head, and these at least remain.

If I walk with the children, Marigold is not with us; there is only Sylvia and Toby. Marigold nearly nineteen is staying with friends in France. She is as charming as ever, and has as little idea of money. I pray as I always have for a husband who has means, or the ability to say 'No'.

Change. The remembrance of Rebecca still haunts me,

though it seems to me that everyone else has forgotten her. I visit her grave in that quiet place where the yew trees cast their shade and the river runs by. Toby sometimes comes with me, and it touches me the way he puts flowers on the grave of the sister he cannot remember. Quite a tall boy now of ten, and usually so lively, he is solemn (true solemn, not fake) and he looks down with pity on the little plot of earth. 'Rotten luck, Rebecca,' he said once. Sylvia, nearly thirteen, is reluctant to visit the grave. I don't know whether this is because it distresses her, or because she finds the visit dull. There are, as always, a lot of things about Sylvia which puzzle me. Her drawing shows more and more power; there is no doubt that she is a talented child. Perhaps she has the complex make-up of the artist. Perhaps that is all.

But then there is Alexander. He is – as so often – not with us. If I look back to some of those early holidays on the island when he would arrive unexpectedly, bringing excitement, it is like looking into a different country. A happier country? In spite of Rebecca, it seems so. At least, a more innocent one.

How do I write of what has happened? To put it baldly, I found a letter. A letter to Alexander, from a woman. A love letter; one could call it nothing else.

I was sorting my books. My books of poetry, the novels of Mr Charles Dickens, the books of flowers, especially those to be found on the island. I took down a book on wine which belonged to Alexander. It was called *The Fruit of the Vine*. As I idly turned the pages, a letter fell out. The letter was old, I could see that, the folding worn, the ink faded. I was about to replace it, when my eye caught the words 'All that we mean and have meant to each other'.

There was no way by which I was not going to read further. No date, simply 'Thursday'.

'My dearest Alexander – I write this because it is true – that is what you are: it expresses all that we mean and have meant to each other. There have been troubles, one can't deny that. But you must try to see the situation from my point of view. I wonder how often *men* do that? I have responsibilities, as you know. I do not, I think, ask for more

82

than is due to me. You know what I mean, what I have given. You must try to—'

I turned the page, but there was no more. The rest of the letter was missing. Simply this page, folded in the book. For how long? I could not know. I returned the page, and the book to its place, and stood in thought. From the open window came the sound of Toby's voice as he encouraged Sylvia to play French cricket.

I could not pretend that I was outraged. I was shocked, as one always is by the uncovering of a secret, the proof that one's world is different from what one has believed. But I was not of sufficient naiveté to be profoundly surprised. A husband who was frequently absent, who had for some time kept to his own room; a husband so often – and certainly of late – in sombre mood, the strange messages that came from Beatrice ...

I lifted my head, as if in sudden recognition. Beatrice. Did *she* know of this attachment – whatever it was? I felt strongly that she did... But how very strange! Beatrice, an accomplice, you might say. I felt myself enclosed in a dark place of uncertainty and deceit. I was not overthrown, I was not heartbroken, but my accustomed moorings were cut.

So where now? I replaced the book on the shelf. When Alexander returned, should I confront him – ask for an explanation? For of course there was much that I did not know. I had a perhaps even stronger impulse to confront Beatrice, for there was a sense in which I thought she saw me as naive, even foolish, as all the deceived must seem. Certainly I could recall on her face that look of superiority which seems to say, 'I know more than you.' Did this other woman fill her idea of an acceptable companion for Alexander more fully than I did?

But then I put this aside as childish, for I was not truly concerned with Beatrice, or what she thought or did not think of me. I knew what I would do, where I was going, and I quickly left the house. As I walked away I could hear Toby's laughter and Sylvia's shout of protest. That was another life.

I decided to walk to the rectory. I lifted my skirt as I followed the path over the Down. The day being so warm, I had no need of a jacket and I wore no hat. The sea far down was a deep un-English blue and the cliffs shone almost white. The gulls cried.

I walked not with anger but with a kind of confidence. It was better to know the truth – or some of the truth. I had of course no idea who the woman was. As I walked through the warm sea-scented air, feeling the sweat on my forehead, I began to wonder about her. No name on the letter, a strong, even unfeminine hand. A woman of character then. Living, I supposed, in London, where Alexander would have for long periods been free to indulge his love, passion, whatever it was...

I bit my lip, feeling an unexpected shaft of jealousy. So one could be jealous where one did not truly love? I was learning new things all the time. Alexander, after all, was the father of my children, the man who had shared, in his own way, my grief over Rebecca.

I walked on, interested in these new discoveries, as the traveller is interested in the habits of an unknown tribe. So this, I was thinking, is what it is like to be deceived, to learn of a secret world, as if a familiar portrait dissolved and showed another beneath. The true portrait. And Alexander? How had it been for him? He carried the burden (for such it must surely be) of deceit; he had to play the father and husband, while all the time... How deeply had he been in love?

Ah, yes; there was the rub. For I knew what love was now. I knew the obsession that set all one's thought upon one person, the place where a different light glittered behind the mundane traffic of the day. I knew the mixture of excitement and pain that changed the ordinary day into a place of discovery. Dangerous discovery, there was no doubt about that.

I paused again, a little breathless now. I had been going at a pace, the pace of one passionately concerned to reach her destination. In other words, to find Piers. And why was I so driven? Because till now I had been shackled, and with this morning's discovery the shackles had been loosened? Very possibly, I thought, as I recovered my breath, for after all, nothing else had changed. My life, my children, my age, the depths of myself were the same. But I had proof, of a kind, of Alexander's infidelity. Did that set me free?'

I walked more slowly now. A breeze lightened the heavy

warmth of the day and was pleasant on my forehead. Looking back I could see how the wind touched the placid glitter of the sea.

This drew my glance with a kind of mesmerizing power, and suddenly, standing there, I was aware of the girl I knew and did not know. Who belonged to the future. She was not walking beside me through darkened and dangerous streets, but standing as I was on the Down above the sea – this sea. And she was in love, I was sure of that. Her presence was so strong that it seemed I might even speak to her, touch her hand. Yet I was aware of the gulf of time that separated us. This brought sadness to me, as lovers feel when the sea divides them. I knew that she would stand here, and though there could be no real threat here on the sunlit turf, I was aware of danger close to her.

Troubled, I walked on. Did one move in more than one corridor of time? Did echoes lie on the air, not only of the past, but of the future? The long future, when all was changed beyond imagining, and one's body dust? The girl would stand here – but for myself? I had no illusions – I had watched Rebecca die; no life was for ever.

And if that was true, what of the present? I walked on towards Piers' house. If darkness waited for us all, then what use was time if one could not love? I went more quickly, holding my skirt free of the ground.

Piers was in his study – that same room where I had come after Rebecca's death. His housekeeper said, 'Mrs St Clair, sir,' and closed the door. If the set of her mouth suggested that the arrival of a woman with blown hair, breathless from walking, was to say the least unexpected, I was not at that moment concerned.

When the door was shut I said, 'I have to talk to you.'

He made a gesture to the chair, but I shook my head. Could we not, I asked, go outside?

'My dear,' he said, 'I have to be here. Something might happen – some disaster. Or at least a parishioner wanting to protest at my last sermon.'

I sat down, reminded that the sane world was at odds with my passionate need to unburden myself.

He leaned forward and took my hands. The gesture was

small, but it brought tears to my eyes. The day that had begun with discovery and brought me headlong to this house seemed to overwhelm me. He said, 'My dear, what's the matter?'

I said with passion, 'Life is too short. We have no certainty about anything. Love is useless. Love can't protect us from death; it couldn't protect Rebecca. There is only a struggle – however good fate may be – a struggle to get through, to learn, and you learn when it's too late. The world is cruel; to the luckiest of us, it is cruel.'

My words ran out. He watched me with quiet interest – too quiet, I thought. He said, 'What's brought this about?'

'Everything. Life. How I feel. How most people feel, I daresay—'

'They lead, Henry Thoreau tells us, lives of quiet desperation.'

'I don't see why they have to be quiet.'

'Tell me what's happened.'

I said I had found a letter. To Alexander. A love letter. Or part of one.

He seemed to think about this. In my present mood, his detachment irked me. At last he said, 'Does that surprise you?'

I opened my mouth once or twice, then said, 'Perhaps not. No, I'm not entirely surprised. But I am ... shocked. Bewildered. Because ... oh, I don't know why.'

He put one hand on mine. 'We can't talk now. A disgruntled parishioner is due in about five minutes. I'll come to you this evening.'

I didn't want to leave him, it was too soon. I glanced about the room and saw his desk piled with papers, the pen laid down. I began to protest, then saw how futile protest would be. Grudgingly obedient, I got to my feet and made my way home, accompanied by the brief unsatisfying memory of our encounter. When the house came into view, for a moment I stood still, preparing myself for a different world.

Piers did not arrive till after nine. Sylvia and Toby were in bed, but not asleep. When I heard the knock, I waited in the living room, trying to calm the beat of my heart.

He came into the room and greeted me as if this were no more than a formal visit. I offered him a chair, trying to match his mood and failing. He said, 'We'll go out. It's a warm evening. I think that'll be best.'

Nanny was upstairs; I told her that I should be out for a little while. Then I took a light shawl, for the day was indeed still warm, and went with a kind of relief, for it was good to be out of the enclosed room. There was still some light at the sea's edge, though the shore was lonely, the rocks darkening above the withdrawing tide.

The words had been pouring through my head almost continuously all day.

'I don't understand. One is taught things as a child, but they're no use. No use at all. No one prepares you for life. No one prepared me for Rebecca's death, no one prepared me for Alexander. No one prepared me for love – what it is, what it can mean.'

He didn't answer at first. He had one hand on my arm, which brought a small comfort. When we came to a seat, up there amongst the gorse on the Down, he motioned me to sit beside him. I turned to look into his face, and he smiled then. 'We've not talked of love – not for some time—'

'But it's true!' I was without caution now, the wide sky and sea, the night air, gave me freedom. 'This is love – what I feel for you. I've not known it before. I'm married and have – had – four children. But this is new. You must know that.'

He put his hand on mine. 'My dearest Isabel. Yes, I know it all, I think. I've loved you from almost the first time we met. Certainly, when you came to me after Rebecca's death – I would have given anything in the world to comfort you, but knew I could not—'

'Then,' I said, interrupting him, 'what is the use of it? If we love each other, and there is only this one life, and there is death at the end of it, what is it for? I have lost Rebecca, and Alexander is unfaithful. Now I have this love which is hardly ever out of my mind – what good is it? *Why*?'

I then sat with my hands together on my lap, as if I tried to distance myself from an outburst which even then sounded to me both childish and absurd. I held my head up, like a mother who tries to deny responsibility for an ill-behaved child.

I glanced quickly at him, then away. He said, 'My darling girl—'

'I am not a girl! I am a woman, approaching middle-age, and I've been talking nonsense. Self-pitying nonsense.'

'My darling girl,' he repeated, 'I have absolutely no answers, as you very well know. If all the theologians have not found an answer to suffering, I'm not likely to be able to do it on a warm night in Freshwater. A hundred sermons won't most likely heal one broken heart. And you don't want a sermon.'

My first was clenched on my knee. 'I want to know how to live with this. To know that Alexander is unfaithful, that you and I have this love for each other. That death can come so early, at any time; that we have no certainty, nothing to make sense of it all.'

That was the human condition, he said with a smile; there were no answers. Except perhaps... He leaned forward, and I saw that he was making a great effort. He spoke of the mystery of pain, of faith, of the words of the mystics, some of which I understood, and some of which were beyond me, and made me impatient.

I said I was not a holy person and that the words of the mystics could do nothing to calm my mind or my spirit.

Yes, he said, again with a smile, he could understand that I didn't find the mystics immediately helpful.

Not helpful at *all*, I said, and found to my discomfort that I was near to tears. He put his arms round me then, which both comforted and alarmed me. Drawing away from him, I looked about me. Day was almost gone and the sea drove heavily to the shore. A light shone from a fishing boat, lonely, some way out. I looked at the darkening horizon where one level rim of light separated sea from sky. I was touched by a sense of illimitable space, which was at once frightening, and yet gave me a kind of calm. Those words of the mystics came to my mind, and I felt a pang of recognition, as if some ancient bell had rung, bringing peace.

I said then, beginning to come to terms with the truth of things as they were, 'I must go home.'

'No, not yet.'

I saw, even in the growing dark, pain and longing in his face. The pain surprised me, and roused a kind of anger. I said, 'I must. It's getting late.' Then the anger calmed and I touched his hand. I said, 'I shall think of you – all the time. Suppose you're not here when I come back to the island?'

'I don't know where I shall be.'

My purpose faltered. 'I can't just walk away from you. Not know where you are – what's happened to you. You might – you might find someone else. Marry again.'

'My dearest love, that would be absurd.'

'You can't possibly know. People change, do things that at one time they wouldn't have believed they could.' I was close to tears again and became angry with myself. I got to my feet and met the sea wind. Light had almost gone and only the faintest gleam showed on the cliff face. He was standing beside me. Heaviness on my heart dragged like a stone. For a moment I could see the long distance of life without him, and with Alexander, for whom I had no love. I began to shiver and he put his arms about me. I held him close to me then, as if I sought rescue. We made promises, avowals, spoke absurdly, as lovers do. Then sharply I remembered my world as it was, and pulled away.

'I must go,' I said again, and when he protested, said, 'I must, I must.'

'But you love me?'

'Oh yes,' I said, 'yes,' and pulled myself away from him. He said my name – 'Isabel' – and there was such love in the word that I longed to turn back. But I went stumbling down the steep path, aware, there on the Down with the sea below, of his pain, a longing equal to my own. I could see the lights of Rosecroft, and went more quickly. I did not look back.

July 24th/25th
The heat continues, and there are many people on the shore. The bathers' voices carry across the water, formless and shrill, signifying happiness.

Alexander is here. He came last night. He arrived late: I heard the sound of the trap and the snuffling of the horse in the still air.

He greeted me with what seemed like absent-minded affection. If I showed any sign of strain he did not seem to be aware of it. He glanced into the children's rooms, but both Sylvia and Toby were asleep. He asked if they were well, and I said, 'Quite well.' That was all.

I woke to the warmth of the new day. My heart and stomach were unsteady, for I knew that I was going to speak to him about the letter, to confront him. I wasn't sure when; I would, I thought, choose the moment – or perhaps it would choose me.

I was quiet at breakfast. Sylvia was complaining that she was bored and when I suggested that she did some painting she said she wasn't any good at it. She grew sulky when I insisted that she was. (She is beginning to have traces of beauty, her figure just developing, her coppery hair loose on her shoulders.) Toby had found a jigsaw puzzle and, fitting in a piece of sky, said, 'I do think sisters are pretty awful sometimes.'

Alexander made no comment. Remembering the letter, I looked at him with curiosity, but this he seemed unaware of. The shadow of the unknown woman lingered in my mind; I at once wanted and did not want to know more of her.

It was not until the afternoon that the chance came to speak to him. The children had gone with Nanny to tea with friends at a house above Afton Down. Alexander was sitting in the garden in a deck chair, his paper on his lap. *Now*, I said to myself, and joined him there.

He looked up as I pushed a chair close to him. 'Marvellous day,' he said. 'Almost too hot.'

I could see the sweat glistening on his forehead; his skin showed a little flush from the sun. He looked handsome, though I could see the grey in his hair. There was light hair too on the backs of his hands. I was, I found, intensely aware of him as a man, the small physical aspects of skin and eye and hand, for I had to believe that he had made love to another woman, skin to skin.

I said, 'I've something to ask you.'

He did not look alarmed, merely lifted his brows. I said, 'I was dusting the books. I opened that one on wine...'

'Really?' He held his paper in abeyance, as if he were bored, and this lighted a small fire in me. I said, 'I found a letter – or rather the page of a letter – inside it. Clearly from a woman – it began "My dearest Alexander".'

His face then changed, showing no expression at all; a visor had come down.

'Naturally enough,' I said, 'I was interested. To say the least. Can you explain it?'

My impression was that behind the mask he was making

rapid calculations, wondering how best to answer me. He glanced once behind him, perhaps to see if anyone was listening, but we were alone in the garden. 'The children are out to tea,' I reminded him.

He said at last, 'I'm sorry you should have seen that.'

'Yes, I expect you are.'

'It was all a long time ago.'

'Really? How long?'

'Oh ... I forget. Some years now.'

I said, 'I think I'd like to know a little more than that.'

He looked at me with guarded antagonism. 'Is it really necessary to go into the past?'

I said I thought in the circumstances it was. I was on the surface quite composed. Underneath some kind of fire burned, of which Piers was perhaps a part.

He said, 'She was a woman I met at one of Clarence's dinner parties –' Clarence was a lawyer whom I had never much cared for '– in town of course, when you were here, on the island.'

'Safely out of the way,' I could not help saying.

He shrugged. 'It was your choice, surely? You've always preferred this place to Russell Square. That's been perfectly plain.'

'The children—' I began.

'The children had – have – a perfectly good Nanny. You could have left them more often than you did.'

Yes, that was true. 'All the same—'

'She was a widow – a young widow. Clarence was dealing with her husband's estate.'

'Her name?' I asked.

He looked aside. 'I see no reason to mention that. As I've said, this is something that belongs to the past. There's really no point in bringing up details now. I have to consider the other people involved—'

'People?' I said sharply. 'Surely there was only one person? This woman?'

He looked at me steadily then: I could not read his expression at all. It came home to me how little I knew of Alexander, despite the years of marriage. A shaft of cold went through me, a touch of things undiscovered.

91

He said, 'Naturally – only her. But she has – had – friends.'

'Friends who knew of your association, you mean?' And then, because the idea came back to me, 'Did *Beatrice* know?'

He was quick on this. 'What a ridiculous idea. How should my sister be concerned in—'

'Your illicit affair? I thought perhaps she might have been.' He couldn't deny, I said, that his relationship with Beatrice was very close. She knew more about his visits to the island than I did: times, details. Of his illness, a little while ago.

'Beatrice is a good friend,' he said. 'She always has been. Since her husband died, she has looked to me for help.'

'Never mind.' Beatrice, at this moment, was not my chief concern. I said, 'This woman – did you love her?'

'I'm not sure I know what love means.'

I drew a breath then, for I thought perhaps this was true, and I felt – in the midst of anger and hurt pride – sorry for him. For I thought *I* knew what love meant: I knew it in truth and pain. I was for a moment overcome by the waste of love, flowing away, leaving a dry land, a dry life. Yet Sylvia and Toby still needed me... Conflicting emotions drove me to anger, and Alexander was there to receive it.

'When you say "some years ago" I don't find that good enough. We're not talking about a visit to forgotten friends, we're talking about making love to some woman unknown to me. *When*, Alexander? When did this happen? And for how long?'

'I don't want questions.'

'But you will *have* questions.' I was strengthened now with anger. 'How old is she? What does the letter mean – "I do not ask for more than is due to me"? Those were her words, I remember them exactly.'

'That is the way women write.' He looked confident, his voice dismissive.

'That is the way they write when they think they have the upper hand.'

A sudden glance suggested that I had touched a nerve. 'You can't possibly know—'

'Precisely. I can't, but I want to. She wrote that she "had responsibilities". What are they? What are they, Alexander?'

He rose from his chair. 'I'm not going to be questioned—'

'But you *are*.'

'Please be quiet, Isabel. There are servants in the house.'

Yes, my voice had risen. But it was not only this that briefly silenced me. I was held both by guilt and fear. Guilt at the thought of Piers, fear of Alexander. For I was afraid of him: he had that quality which is hard to define but is instantly recognisable – the power to create fear. All the same I persisted, 'What *are* her responsibilities?'

'I've told you – it's all in the past. I can't remember what she was referring to. Women write all sorts of things – they exaggerate.' I began to speak again, but he interrupted. 'I've nothing more to say. The whole thing is over.'

He turned and strode back into the house. I stayed in the garden alone. The wash of the sea was louder now that our voices were silenced. I was still shaking a little from anger, and the frustration of Alexander's refusal to answer me. I seemed to have made a great effort and achieved little save his antagonism.

But there was more to know, and some time, I told myself, I would discover it.

July 26th

Today the weather has broken; the night was full of lashing rain. I lay listening to it, for after the confrontation with Alexander, I found it hard to sleep. By morning the rain had lessened, but the sky was overcast, the sea grey, slapping against the rocks.

The pattern of the day was the same – but of course it was at heart entirely changed. The knowledge that lay between Alexander and me had altered the house as surely as if some dark magic had altered its proportions.

As soon as I could, I went outside. The rain had become nothing more than a damp mist; there was even brightness at the far rim of the sea, as if a strip of man-made light had been drawn there. I looked at this bay which I loved, and saw that it could not offer me its usual peace. That overcast sky echoed the confusion of my own mind: of Alexander's infidelity, of my longing to go to Piers. However, I did not turn that way. I made for Beatrice's house, but before I reached it I saw her coming towards me. She wore a light mackintosh cape and carried a

93

basket. Face to face with her, I stood still. I had gone on an impulse, but now was at a loss for words.

I saw her eyes go over me, as if she made a judgement on my appearance, which was no doubt in some disarray. I said I wished to speak to her, not being sure that this was quite true. She seemed to hesitate, then turned and led me back into the house.

'I was on my way to church to do the flowers,' she said, taking off her gloves, 'but I can go later.'

I could not quite gauge her mood, for she seemed to spark with a kind of triumph. 'Well?' she asked, and I said abruptly that I had discovered something about Alexander which had distressed me. I watched her face, but it showed little; merely a lift of her brows.

'Alexander has had an affair,' I said, feeling the anger of frustration, for I could see already that she was not going to respond with sympathy, or indeed surprise. I said with passion, 'I found a letter from a woman. In loving terms. He didn't deny it.'

She looked beyond me to the window. 'What can one say? Men are men.'

'You don't condemn him?'

'I'm sorry that it should be so—'

'You knew nothing of it?'

'*I*?' She looked at me then. 'How should I know anything? Would my brother discuss such things with me – a woman of the Church?'

I thought about it. There was something that troubled me, that did not quite ring true. I said, 'I have thought that you – you had a secret. Something that I didn't know.'

'My dear Isabel, that is nonsense. How should I have secrets? Indeed – it is not *I* who have secrets!'

'I – I don't know what you mean.'

'Ah! Perhaps not.' Yes, Beatrice was truly in command. She went on, 'I sometimes go for a walk after dinner – summer evenings can seem long when you live alone. And until today, it has been hot, even airless.'

I sat still in this alien room. The flash of understanding left me silent.

'The other evening,' she said, 'I walked on the Down. I expected to see no one.'

In the silence I heard the clock tick and the drum of the sea wind at the window. I was for a brief moment lost in that encounter on the cliff's top, with the dark sea below us, and the passion that enclosed me and shut all thought of the outside world away.

Beatrice. Somewhere close by. I tried to recall what words had passed between Piers and myself. What had she heard?

I waited. She was not going to satisfy my curiosity. 'I did not naturally stay long. I simply saw – saw an embrace.'

I looked at her, still silent. I had an impulse to say forcefully, 'Yes, I love him; we love each other – can you understand that?' but something in her face prevented me. 'He was giving me comfort,' I said, and then with the sense of having a weapon of my own, 'For Alexander's defection.'

Her face did not change, but her silence told me that I had struck home. She said at last, 'That was surely unnecessary – to tell Mr Malleson—'

'Unnecessary! Is that not what a priest is for? To listen to the disasters and distress of those in his care? Why should I not have told him? He will tell no one, he is bound by his calling.'

'His calling,' Beatrice said. 'Yes ... but perhaps that is not as certain as it might be. To many of us his ministry gives an uncertain sound.'

Angered, I said, 'He is a good man!'

Beatrice rose to her feet. 'No doubt you would believe so.' And before I could say more, 'I have an appointment. I shall be late.'

Silent, I rose too and went ahead of her. We parted, there in the road. I was left with a sensation of discomfort. More than discomfort, perhaps; a kind of fear. Beatrice had power, just as Alexander had power. And both knew more than they were prepared to tell me; I was clear about that.

I turned back the way I had come. I would not, I told myself when I reached the house, look too far ahead. Rebecca's death had taught me how futile it was to count even on the next day. I would hold on to this moment, where a misty sun brightens over the sea and the gulls scream with a kind of angry triumph.

Chapter 11
Kate – 1940

Kate put the journal aside, lit a cigarette, and glanced at her
watch. Reading had absorbed her; by now Perdita would be
(with luck) in Cumberland. This place, Kate thought, seemed
empty without her. She glanced again at the pile of books.
Despite having the look of material for the scrapheap, they
were powerful with life. Isabel had become a friend – a coun-
sellor, perhaps? For these, to say the least, were difficult
times. Bloody difficult, Kate thought, sooner or later, someone
will come – you can't duck authority for ever. The ATS will
come with sniffer dogs. And you can't escape the prospect
before you – that large question of the child. Charles' child.
Not much time for that one. You have to make up your mind.
No one knows except Perdita – and perhaps, she thought, with
another glance at the journals – Isabel?

The echo of Perdita's lively presence lingered in the room,
seeming to blend with the echo of Isabel, on the island, so
long ago. Perdita in the Lakeland village, with the cold mountain air, free from the threat of bombs. Perdita with her two
children, and Bronwen Stannard, her mother-in-law. Bronwen,
whose husband, Lionel had quit the home when Gerald, her
son, was eight years old, so that all Bronwen's hopes centred
on him. Hopes of a marriage of some splendour, St
Margaret's, Westminster, crossed swords, even trumpets...
Instead, she got Perdita. A thoroughly good girl, but earning
four pounds a week in the Civil Service, and with a widowed
mother of uncertain mind.

Perdita, unable to deny Bronwen's edict that the children
must come and stay for the duration in the safety of the Lake

District. The two of them, Bronwen and Perdita, the children in bed, listened nightly to the news and heard of 'heavy raids on enemy territory', waiting in the quiet room in case the words 'reported missing' or 'failed to return' should monstrously echo there.

I'd like her back, Kate thought. Hope the boy's all right. And as for me? Well, I have to do something. There's a war on, after all.

She glanced aside, as if she looked into the featureless landscape of destruction, not only close at hand, but across the countries of Europe. Torn and broken houses, men and women in the ragged clothes of the refugee, bewildered children, carried or dragged along in the desolate and threatened cavalcade. War. Making small her own predicament.

Resigned, she sat before her desk and wrote to her Senior Commander in the ATS, offering sackcloth and ashes (though these, she thought, would not be enough for overstaying her leave). There were what you might call 'mitigating circumstances' perhaps, for after all, there was still the ceremony of the ashes. But the time of her leave had run out, and punishment was waiting, which she would accept. Not much choice, have I? she thought.

Having written the letter, she looked at it with a lack of enthusiasm, as if it were a poor page of manuscript. She could remember a questionnaire at some point of her training, where the question was asked, 'How would you describe yourself?' She had written, 'A natural sinner, a martyr to unproductive remorse, a prey to over-anxiety. Always noticeable, frequently wrong, seldom negative.' This had produced no comment.

She sealed the letter, pushed it a little way from her on the desk, and thought again about Isabel. There was, she thought, a kind of comfort there. Isabel with her lost child and her love for that nice reverend ... What *did* happen, she wondered. What came of it...

A sound from the hall recalled her to the present: the flap of the letter box.

She didn't immediately move, for what could the wartime post bring of any interest, now there could be no letter from Charles?

After some moments she went into the hall and picked up

the letter. It had not come through the post; it had been delivered by hand. She opened the front door, but the long corridor with its closed doors was empty. The letter was addressed to her – 'Kate Lewis' – in a strong hand. Returning to the room she opened it and read:

'Dear Kate Lewis,

(I don't know if you are married or not; but I address you in your maiden name.)

I have wanted to get in touch with you, but thought it best to approach you by letter first. I am against sudden appearances myself; I like due warning.

But I think we should meet, and in the present circumstances, when each day is so uncertain, I think – if you agree – that we should meet soon.

In case you wonder who I am, I saw you at Isabel's funeral.

My name is Jasper Vye. I don't know if it means anything to you. But I knew your grandmother Isabel.

How do I end this letter?

In hope, I think.

J.V.'

Kate went at once to the window and looked out into the daytime street. The people who passed below were all strangers and she couldn't know if the deliverer of the letter was among them.

'Jasper Vye.' The name of the young man on the island, whom Isabel had seen talking to Alexander. There was an address and telephone number – somewhere in Chelsea. 'I saw you at Isabel's funeral.'

'Well, now,' Kate said aloud, taking another cigarette, seeing the male figure who had so rapidly vanished. Oh yes, she would call him, make some contact. But first she would get in touch with Perdita.

With a small surge of excitement, as if some clue were fitting into place, she lifted the telephone.

Chapter 12
Isabel – 1900

July

Much changes, but not the bay. We have gaslight at Rosecroft instead of the oil lamps and candles. Nanny is still with us, though there are no children for her to care for. Marigold is married, and Sylvia, nearly nineteen, is at art school: she has been accepted by the 'Slade', founded by the late Felix Slade, and this is an honour, I understand, under the awesome Professor Tonks.

Only Toby is with me. I get – as ever – much pleasure from his company, for he still seems to look on life as an interesting adventure which one need not take too seriously.

I don't know how much he knows about Alexander. His attitude to his father is well-tempered, but I can catch a certain reserve. And Alexander himself, who was always so proud of his son, looks on him now with a kind of wariness, as if he tries to read behind Toby's easy words some different truth.

But Toby of course is growing into manhood, he too will soon be away. He has friends on the island: young men of his own age, and a little older. (Girls too: I see them talk to him, heads a little to one side.) The boys love sailing, as Toby does – he talks with endless enthusiasm, as all converts do. I see him go off in jacket and white trousers and canvas shoes. He goes with a run and a leap of excitement, turns to wave and then is off. I have sometimes been down to the shore to watch them: I can feel something of the excitement, the open wind in the swelling sails. I watch the boat travel with winged grace over the water until its shape grows small. When he returns home his skin is whipped into colour and his hair is tousled by the sea wind; he is a young man intoxicated. 'It's like riding in the sky,' he said once.

Yes, he has a gift for happiness. Often I remember Rebecca: she would have been a young woman. I have counted every birthday – a young woman of twenty-three. But those are words, the arithmetic of logic. Rebecca is the child who ran on the shore and played with the seaweed, who is gone for ever. I do not forget her. Alexander never mentions her – I don't know how much he remembers her in his heart. Toby, having been told of her birthday, remembers it and writes messages to me – nothing flowery, which is not in his nature, but just her name and the date, the 14th of May, and 'Love from Toby' at the bottom. He asks me questions about her sometimes, without embarrassment, which gives me a little ease. Toby is untidy, impetuous, but he has the gift of kindness.

Marigold is married to a business man, Conrad Lewis. He is a hard man, I think – or at any rate, he makes no effort to charm. He was much attracted by Marigold's beauty – her coppery hair and elegant figure. But he had quickly grown impatient with her extravagance and her unpunctuality – Marigold was always late and Conrad alarmingly punctual. They travelled, lived for a time in Paris. Letters came from Marigold, usually complaining about some failure of her husband. She hoped for a child, she said, but so far had not conceived. For this, too (with no particular reason that I could fathom), she seemed to blame her husband. I hoped very much for the child, for I thought there might be some happiness there.

And Sylvia? She could still plunge from gaiety to despair, but she enjoyed her days at the Slade School; I had hopes that her talent, which was considerable, would play its part in giving balance to her life.

Today there is no wind; not a day for sailing, Toby says. He is out with his friends... Having accomplished my household tasks, I took the familiar path up on the Down. And there I remembered my dream of last night. A dark dream, such as I'd known before, but this time the danger was not in city streets: it was in open country, dreadful country, with stunted trees, ploughed land and lights that lifted above the cursed place and terribly defined it, with the bodies lying there. In my dream I walked among the bodies, but saw none that I knew. Somewhere out of sight there was a sound of weeping, the weeping of many women.

Standing there I drew my hands over my face, as if to wipe the memory away. I looked to the wide expanse of the sea; slowly the dark images faded. I was myself again, on the familiar path, and I lifted my skirt and walked on towards Piers' house.

His house, though no longer the rectory, was in sight of the bay. There is much to tell and I am not sure where best to begin. No, I am not ashamed to write of it, but I want to get events in their right order.

Piers had left the Church. Or he had left the Ministry. He had found a way of solving – or beginning to solve – his dilemma of faith. He wrote books which startled and in some cases offended the conventional churchgoer, but which found a lively reception with those of a liberal mind – who, like Mr Matthew Arnold, were conscious of the wind of doubt. These books, and visiting the poor, the sick and the distressed, kept him fully occupied. And the royalties from the books, and a small income from a family inheritance, provided him with enough to live on. A simple life, perhaps, but though no ascetic, he didn't greatly trouble about food and drink or what he should wear. He had an absent-minded way of looking at such things, as if they were irrelevant interruptions of some more interesting purpose.

We became lovers. (I write that now, but the words surprise me, if the fact does not.) I shall tell of how it came about a little later. It was some time after I learned of Alexander's defection. Our love for each other had endured, unfulfilled, for a long time. But it was not a pallid acceptance of denied passion – we desired each other as men and women in love do. I had slept alone for a long time; Alexander kept to his room. My dreams were sometimes powerful and robust. I had small sense of guilt; we had served a long apprenticeship.

I was not troubled, as he was, by his distant, uncertain, yet still powerful God. I was free from a sense of other-worldliness. The enduring memory of Rebecca put me at a distance from any kind of belief. I was, in short, more at peace with our love than he was. I accepted it, with its power, its longing and its

101

comradeship; sometimes its fun. More at peace, but not less loving. He loved me with a devotion which at once humbled and delighted me. With his love he created a person who was not myself, who was more admirable, more beautiful, in every way more to be revered. I said once, 'But I have so many faults! I don't really like myself very much.'

'Oh dear!' We were walking by the shore and he smiled down at me. 'We'll spend an evening in discussion of your faults. Some time. Not just now.' He created a place of extreme certainty. 'I shall always love you,' he said. 'Always.' He looked at the tranquil wash of sea on shingle. 'I don't know what "always" means. But whatever it is, I shall love you.'

Yes, I believed him. I thought how many times those words had been spoken in how many languages – spoken and proved false. But these I believed. His words were not extravagant; he spoke as a man speaks on a subject he has studied deeply, with an easy command. He spoke of the past, of his wife and the dead child. 'I loved her very much,' he said, 'but I was young, and the time was short. Now I'm not young any more. One loves differently in later years.'

'Differently – but not less passionately,' I said.

'No,' he said, after a little pause. 'That is not less. Whatever Hamlet said about the heyday in the blood.'

When I parted from him I felt at once elated and sorrowful. For there were the children (scarcely children any more – but Toby still needed my care and my love). Then there was Alexander.

We lived a strange life (though perhaps no stranger than many husbands and wives: marriage is secret territory). As I have said, we slept apart – there was no question about that, though no word was spoken. There had been one evening when Alexander had drunk well at dinner (we were in London, not on the island) and he wandered across the room and stood behind my chair. I could smell the scent of his cigar. The fire burned low. He let one hand touch my head, then gently slip down my cheek, lingering there. 'You look very pretty tonight, my dear,' he said. I drew my breath and very slightly moved from his hand. There was no need to do more. I heard his laugh, as if his words had been of no significance; then he moved away and, yawning, glanced at his watch.

For the rest, we lived a life of apparent conformity. From time to time we discussed events in the outside world. There was of course the war in Africa, with the Boers: the news of the relief of Mafeking (Sylvia told me that the art school erupted in excitement and the students scrambled on to a horse bus and travelled cheering through the streets). Alexander and I talked of such things amiably enough. If we disagreed about the Boers, he rode this with ease, clearly looking on me as a woman with sentimental ideas about Boer farmers. This didn't greatly trouble me, for Alexander could not cause me pain now. I was so much in love that he was like a stranger in my life.

A stranger – but for one thing. I sometimes caught sight of him, standing motionless, hands behind his back, looking from the window. Unaware of me, and therefore vulnerable, as the spied-on always are, he stood brooding, and the expression on his face disturbed me. He looked as if he faced an enemy or, at any rate, something that made him afraid.

I did not question him. Various constraints prevented me: we were after all no longer on terms when we spoke deep truth to one another. And there was a sense in which I did not want to know what it was that troubled him. Perhaps he was only brooding on past unhappiness: that, in middle-age, is easily done.

Come July, I returned to the island. There was no argument about my going: those days were long past. Toby had been invited by a friend from school, Guy Leighton, to stay in Bosham, where they would be sailing. So I travelled alone. I had no thought of Alexander as the ferry left the shore at Lymington and approached the island. The familiar shape of the Down grew from a summer mist, the water slipped fanwise from our travelling. Yes, I had always loved the island, but now it contained a more powerful lure. I stood by the ferry's rail and watched the beloved place come closer. My fellow travellers, if they observed me at all, must have seen only a woman, no longer in her first youth, content to be visiting the island. Heightened colour they would ascribe to the sea wind.

The house and Nanny received me. Rosecroft, with all its echoes: the children's voices, Rebecca's voice; Alexander's

103

voice, in the days before the division came between us... How quickly, I thought, it all passes. And Piers? I had written to tell him of my coming. He would know why I had written and he would be both elated and disturbed. I could understand the disturbance, but the strong wind of love carried me forward. I had no doubts. It seemed to me that I had waited all my life for this. I had borne my children and loved them, but until now I had not known love for a man. But now – now it was here and, though I was no longer young, it possessed me entirely.

As soon as I had changed from my dusty travelling clothes, I set out on foot from the house. I walked with purpose, without fear. Yet strangely, as I walked over the wide space of the Down, the sea wind playing with my skirt, I felt that touch of a different time, of a young woman who walked this path, as I did, with thoughts of a lover. The sensation was strong, so that for a moment the cliffs and the sea and the familiar houses took on the look of things not immediately seen, but remembered. Remembered from a changed time. I was powerfully aware of her, and of a need to speak to her, across the gulf that separated us. She seemed to move in a little tent of sorrow and I walked more quickly because she troubled me. I did not want to think of sorrow; now, I told myself, was the hour for lightness of heart, a span of joy snatched from the passing time.

I had reached his house. Now my heart raced and I took off my hat and wiped my forehead. He opened the door himself, and I caught on his face a look of deep sweet relief, as if he had doubted whether I would come. I had never seen that look on Alexander's face – nor on any man's.

I moved swiftly into the house. I gave one glance towards the kitchen parts, but he gave a small shake of his head. We were alone. So I followed him into the living room as if I sought shelter. There I let my hat fall and flung myself into his arms.

When we drew apart I saw the longing in his face, but the doubt also. He said, 'Not now. Not yet.'

I glanced all round the room with a kind of impatience, but then I smiled and picked up my hat from where it had fallen. I said, 'Very well, then.'

I spoke lightly but perhaps he caught some shade of disappointment for he took me by the arms and said, 'You know how much I want you and love you. More than anything on earth. For the rest of my life – however long that is.'

I looked into his face and noticed the first signs of ageing, the lines scored more deeply, a shadow below the cheekbones where the flesh was thinner. Yes, I knew the love was real, but I knew also that he felt a weight of guilt. I said, 'Your God still watches over you. Tells you what to do.'

'You doubt what I say?'

'No. But what *I* say is true.'

He looked over my shoulder. 'Perhaps. I don't preach any more, I don't tell children – or adults either – what they are to believe. But there is a pull that I can't escape...'

'Then you'd rather I went away from you? Went back to my house, to my life, and lived it through without you? So that we never met again – or only as strangers?'

He said, 'Oh, my beloved Isabel. To lose you would be like losing life – surely you know that? To go on without you would mean that life would be empty and stale. Not worth living. Nothing – none of the books here, or – or the light on the sea, would mean anything to me. I would be better dead.'

I faced him then and met the truth of what he said. I felt triumphant and at the same time afraid, because this declaration of love seemed a large thing, almost beyond my understanding, like death. Like Rebecca's death.

I had only one answer. 'Then I will return this evening,' I said without shyness, as if we spoke of some formal engagement. 'I will come back.'

As I returned the way I had come, my head was full of words, and I scarcely saw the Down and the scabious and the cropped grass and the sea beyond, green and lively with morning. Yes, he knew some guilt, and at heart perhaps I did too. But I protested, as if I spoke to some figure of authority, 'What do you ask of me? You have Rebecca; Alexander has another love. I am no longer young, and I have met love as I have never understood it before, nor will again. Time is running out; there is only this little while. Toby still needs me, and I will be there for him. But he will go, and there will be the long dry time of growing older, with the fires burning low, of a path not taken, a love lost.'

Yes, perhaps I tried to justify myself, but I believed my

outpouring. I believed that to turn from Piers was wrong...
Did I think about his God? He was a distant shadow. He had
taken Rebecca; he had, it seemed to me, small love for his
creatures. They were entitled, surely, to take joy where they
could find it, where it could do no harm.

Just this one short life. And the chance of a deep happiness,
a fulfilment which, whatever came after, would burn like fire
in my memory. And Piers? I could perhaps ease his doubts; I
could meet him in a country of delight – for a little while. And
the future? I couldn't see into that; there was simply 'Now'.

The day, which passed slowly, did not seem quite real. I
made visits, wrote letters – yet it was someone else who did
these things, not wholly myself. My true self was ahead,
racing towards evening.

Light stayed long above the sea; the shape of a quarter moon
showed on the pale sky. I had no taste for an evening meal. As
the summer dusk spread over the Down, I set out from the
house. As I walked I glanced back and saw the lamps casting a
glow from the windows. Rosecroft, the familiar house that had
seen so much of my life here on the island. But I was turning
my back on it now.

Dusk was draining colour from grass and tree. I caught sight
of a young woman, her long white skirt washed through with
darkness as if with ink. Despite the gloom I recognised her:
Meg Sanderson, a wild girl with abundant red hair, blown by
the wind. I had seen her sometimes walking barefoot on the
shore. She served at other times at the local inn. But now she
walked with a young man whose head was bent towards her – I
could not see his face, and neither of them would notice me.
And if they did, they would show no interest; it would not
cross their minds that I was as deep in love as they – perhaps
more so. The young believe that love is their exclusive territory, but they are wrong.

I went more quickly. The sound of the sea was distant, quiet
with evening. The sound had a mixture of magic and melancholy.

I had reached the house. There was no need to give more
than the slightest knock on the door. Quickly he opened it and
I slipped inside, as if I escaped a pursuer.

Not many words were spoken. We had made a promise, we

had pledged our love, and this was loving. The house was empty and silent. An oil lamp made a small pool of light on the landing of the stair. I was not afraid of the room, of the bed there.

After he had taken me in his arms I sat, removing the light scarf from my shoulders. He was looking at me with a smile that had a trace of sadness in it. He said, 'You look quite lovely.'

'Oh, Piers, I am not a young girl... But if you say so, I'll accept that I have some beauty left.'

Yes, he said; yes, I had that. He knelt before me, and his hands as they stroked my face were trembling. I had this great need – absurd perhaps – to protect him, as I had once protected the children. It was not difficult to slip from our clothes – or it seemed not to be so. Perhaps the drive of longing dissolved the awkwardness of undoing corset and petticoat. Before I slipped between the sheets, I had a moment to be grateful that I had not grown fat with later years.

I had forgotten that a man becomes someone other when he loses himself in the force of loving – close, part of you. So it had been with Alexander, but this was not Alexander. Piers did not love as Alexander had, with the violence of a man making a conquest. Gentleness tempered passion; he was saying, 'Oh, my love, my very dearest love,' and I answered him: there was no difference between us. It was only when it was over that I felt the tears spill: when he asked me why I wept, I said I didn't know.

But when we were dressed, he said, 'My darling, at first it was you who was able to shut down my doubt. Now I feel that I own the world because I have you, yet you were the one who cried.'

I wiped my face. We were sitting together on the sofa, his arm about my shoulders. I smiled and said, 'I suddenly lost hope.' When he asked hope in what? I said again I didn't know. In the future, perhaps.

'Yes,' he said, 'we have to think about that.'

I felt a chill, there in the warm room. It was true my early confidence had faded. Words about sadness after the act of love occurred to me. I said, 'You mean a parting from Alexander?'

'Surely not impossible?'

Yes, certainly our roles had reversed. Now Piers was in command, and I saw confusion ahead. Yes, I loved him, but I was married, a whole life lived as partner to Alexander. There was, I thought, no love between us, yet there was a mysterious bond, formed by the years, small triumphs, failures, most of all birth of the children. Piers was a widower who had found his love.

'There are the children,' I said.

'Scarcely children now. The girls are grown up—'

'Toby is only sixteen.'

'He will have his life. You – we – would be there for him.'

'Alexander is his father.'

Piers rose in a sudden movement. I watched him and saw that he had changed: he was no longer the man who had held me close and become part of me. He was almost a stranger.

He said, 'We both know about Alexander. You've been apart for a long time. There's no love there.'

I said, No.

'We belong to each other. What has this evening been if it has not proved that?'

I shook my head, not in denial but in confusion. I felt the tears rise again, and was impatient with them. I controlled myself and said could we not please just rest in this moment? In the lamplit room, with the dark outside and the distant sound of the sea? (This is what I meant, if I did not use those exact words.) He turned to me with a kind of anger; for a moment I felt the cold of rejection. I wanted to plead with him, but I found no words. At last I said, my voice thin, 'Please give me time. I love you very much. With all my heart ... please give me time.'

I waited, then saw his face soften. He put his hands on my shoulders. 'I've distressed you, my darling. I'm sorry. I never want to hurt you; you mean more to me than anything in the world. My dear love – you're crying. Please don't.'

Again I wiped my face, and rose to my feet. The room had the feel of a late hour; candles on the mantelpiece burned low. It was time for me to leave. As I made a movement from him he said, 'No, not yet,' with such longing that my heart misgave me. He took me in his arms and I lost myself in the warmth of comfort. But then a clock sounded and I withdrew again. It was late, I said; I had to go. Accepting this he said, 'But I shall see you again? Soon?'

'Yes,' I said, already moving from him, 'soon.' He said he would see me to my house, but I shook my head. 'Someone might see us,' I said, and was aware of duplicity, of things to be hidden.

In the end he let me go alone. I went over the dark silent ways above the night sea. I was not the same woman who had come towards his house, in confidence, in the summer dusk. Now I knew doubt and fear, as well as the fulfilment of love. I was aware of danger, and as I walked there alone, I was also most strangely aware of company, of that other girl, in difficult love in a different and future time.

Chapter 13
Isabel – 1900

August

I have come to no resolution. I am deep in love, but I look on the shore and the children who play there, the tall cliffs where the evening light falls, and know that innocence has gone from it all. Piers is patient with me – so far. But there is tension between us and I can't know how long his patience will last. Sometimes, wakeful in the small hours, I am afraid.

I was glad that today was the day of Toby's arrival – his coming filled the house with expectancy. Nanny was delighted, busy with preparations. She is old now, but remembers so much of the past, and now that Marigold and Sylvia have left home, she focuses all her affection on Toby. Her watery eyes look on him with love, the love that knows, because she is old, it must soon say goodbye.

He arrived about four o'clock. I heard the coach – I was already in the garden. I rose quickly, anxious to shut away all thoughts of Piers. Indeed, Toby's arrival entirely occupied me; I was so very glad to see him. As he got down from the coach and saluted old Dick, the driver (whom of course he knew well), I was able to observe him while he was as yet unaware of me. Sun and sea had bleached his hair; he stood tall, as Alexander did, and I looked on him with pride. I called his name, and he lifted an arm and came towards me.

At first I thought his greeting was the same as it always had been. He hugged me, and said, 'Hello, Mama,' and walked easily beside me towards the house. He greeted Nanny with an exuberant affection, which she delighted in. 'Welcome back, Mr Toby. Oh, it's so good to see you again.'

110

Yes, there was love there; love rooted deep in the past when she had taken him by the hand as he stumbled over the pebbles on the shore.

I waited for him to join me in the garden, as I knew he liked to unpack and accustom himself to his room on his own, without an intruding voice. When he came to sit beside me I asked how he had enjoyed his time with the Leightons? I was surprised at his silence; it was as if he'd not heard me. But then he said, yes, he'd enjoyed it. They had had good sailing weather. Guy had taught him a lot; he was learning more and more about the craft. Then he fell silent, absently plucking at the grass.

I knew better than to prod him with questions. Toby, for all his good nature, had his moods of secrecy, especially now that he had come to adolescence. I did not chatter about the island either, for it would have sounded false. He said at last that Guy would be coming to Freshwater – they planned to sail round Hatherwood Point and Alum Bay.

'That's splendid,' I said. 'Will he stay with us for a night or two?'

He said, 'Yes, perhaps.' Then he asked, 'Will Father be here?'

A little surprised, I said merely that I couldn't be sure; the pattern was as it had always been – he might arrive at any time. Toby nodded; then said, 'Did you ever know a man called Duvane?'

I tried to think back. It was at least an unusual name and had a faint, it seemed to me sinister, familiarity, as if it had been an unpleasing character in some long-forgotten book. Then suddenly the memory sprang. Mrs Duvane. That evening when I had been summoned to town: the memory was clear because I had not fully understood the occasion, and I remembered also Mrs Duvane's nephew who had talked so seriously with Alexander. 'Yes,' I said. 'I remember a dinner with Mrs Duvane. Alexander told me to entertain her with talk of the children, but I found it hard to get a word in. Yes, I remember her.'

'And the man? Gilbert Duvane?'

'That must have been her nephew.' I glanced at Toby and he nodded, as if I had made something clear. But it was not clear to me. 'How d'you know about them?' I asked. 'The Duvanes?'

He frowned, not quite at ease. 'Well, Guy's parents had friends in to dinner. His father's a solicitor; one of the dinner party was too. When the women had left the table, Guy and I stayed on. The talk mostly went over my head and I began to feel sleepy – they'd let me have some wine.'

I could see the picture: candles on the table, cigar smoke, male adult conversation across the dessert plates, the boy drowsy with unaccustomed wine.

'They were talking about money – how people could lose it on investments. Things like 'half-per-cent Indian stock'. I think Guy was as bored as I was. And then his father said something like "Look at Gilbert Duvane. When his aunt died." And then there was a kind of silence.'

His aunt. Mrs Duvane. That pleasant, somewhat untidy, talkative lady, gone. I said, 'A silence?'

'They were both looking at me. I couldn't imagine why. I thought I must have fallen asleep and snored or something. Then Guy's father said, "Your name's Toby, isn't it – Toby St Clair?" And the other man looked at Guy's father, as if he'd just jabbed him with a pin. I felt myself going red and they changed the subject with a rather false kind of cheerfulness.'

I smiled, reflecting that young men of Toby's age were no longer children. 'Was that all?' I asked.

'Not quite. I was going through the hall when I heard Guy's father and his friend talking in the library. It's that kind of house. The door was open. Guy's father said, "So far Gilbert Duvane hasn't been able to prove anything. But I wouldn't care to be in Alexander St Clair's shoes." What d'you think he meant?'

A sensation like a twist of wire went through my stomach. I said, 'I don't know.' My thoughts scurried, going back and back, gathering odd moments of disquiet: most vividly those glimpses of Alexander, sunk in morose reverie. And the long murmuring talks with Beatrice on some subject unknown to me...

Toby said, 'It seemed an odd remark. Why on earth wouldn't he want to be in Father's shoes? Is there something wrong?'

Quite possibly, I thought, but I wanted to reassure him, and

112

put my hand on his. 'I don't expect so. Men talk after dinner – wine loosens their tongues.'

'Made me want to go to sleep,' he said.

That was all we said about it at the time.

August 15th

When I woke, I saw there had been rain in the night; the air was still damp, the sea grey. I much wanted to tell Piers of the "odd remark", but I didn't want to leave Toby until Guy joined him.

However, he seemed cheerful enough as he walked towards the shore. The sea, washing the sand and shingle, was taking the first shine of sunlight. Toby stood beside me, drawing in the scent of weed and salt. The tide being low, the strange table rock stood clear, weed-draped, in the still water. I said, 'Your Aunt Beatrice never liked that part of the shore.'

'Really? Why not?'

I told him about the rock; that she had said it looked like an altar for sacrifice – or something of that kind.

Toby looked towards it. 'Honestly? Can't say it ever occurred to me. Suppose it is rather an odd shape...' He smoothed his hair against the sea wind. 'I do love the sea. When I'm away from it I feel lost. I don't like towns. Perhaps I could be a sailor. How would Father like that, d'you think?'

I laughed. 'Not very well, I imagine. He wants you to go into the firm.'

'I know. It's the last thing *I* want, you know that. Try to talk him out of it, won't you, Ma?'

I said I would do what I could. A trace of unease had come in with mention of Alexander. We walked on, up on to Afton Down. Below us the Arch rock stood like a tall cathedral ruin; the sea was turning from grey to blue-green, with small shards of light showing on the calm water. The gulls swooped and screamed. We came to the small monument in memory of the child lost from the cliff's edge. 'Poor kid,' Toby said; and then, 'Shall we go and see Rebecca's grave? Take some flowers?'

I don't know what made him say that. Simply, I suppose, this lost child, so long ago. We walked back through the village to the church, buying flowers on the way – summer flowers, drooping a little. The graveyard was empty but for ourselves, in a sunlit silence. Just the flutter of bird's wing and a stirring of the grass. Toby put the flowers in a container which I kept near the grave. He did it with simple efficiency; I don't know why it seemed like a ritual.

I read the words on the stone: 'Rebecca, beloved daughter of Alexander and Isabel St Clair. Safe in the arms of Jesus.' These last words had been Alexander's choice, not mine. I had no certainty that Rebecca was safe; I only knew that there was still a raw wound within me, a kind of anger, a sense of so much love gone to waste... But then I looked over the grave-yard in the summer quiet, and the vast distances of time commemorated there made my anger a small thing; I was aware again of the long future, of some sorrow not my own. What whisper did I hear, and who spoke it...? No, there was no one but ourselves, and the small task was done.

Toby and I walked away together, leaving the place to its quiet.

August 17th

This morning Alexander returned. He arrived just before midday. I greeted him with polite reserve, which was my habit now. At times I regretted this, for there had been some happi-ness once, and the birth of children. But all that was changed.

Toby greeted him with caution. Alexander had greatly wanted a son and had doted on Toby as a child. But now, as Toby grew into adolescence, Alexander would sometimes argue with him, speak with caustic authority, from which Toby would turn away in bruised silence. I was not at ease when they were together, for although Toby never took up an argument, I could feel his hurt. Alexander could fill a room with his pres-ence and his mood. I had grown used to that now, but when Toby was there I could feel the pricking on my nerves.

'So you're sailing now?' Alexander said. 'Hope you know what you're doing. Not a sport for amateurs.'

I saw Toby flush. 'Yes, I think I know quite a lot about it. Guy certainly does.'

'Young men tend to think they know everything. There's a lot to be learned. I sailed myself as a young man, but I took no risks.'

Toby didn't reply. Alexander watched him go from the

room. Toby didn't go in anger, but I saw Alexander's face set. When Toby had gone, he shrugged and said, 'Don't know why the boy never talks to me now. We used to be such friends.'

The words caught me suddenly before I could protest in Toby's defence. 'We used to be such friends' – the words touched that most sensitive of nerves, the sense of love, of happiness gone. Yes, Alexander, despite his readiness to ride a high horse, had some place in his heart which Toby could wound, and I felt a pang of sympathy for him.

It was later when Toby was out with Guy Leighton that I made up my mind to speak to Alexander about Gilbert Duvane. The small mystery nagged at me and when we had finished dinner I said, 'Let's go outside. It's still warm.' Alexander gave a grunt of assent. I found that since we had grown apart he more readily agreed to any small suggestion. We did not, perhaps, any longer care enough for each other to argue.

The garden was dusky, but with a trace of light on the horizon. I could smell the sea. Alexander strolled beside me, smoking his cigar. I could feel his strong masculinity, but it was removed from me. The man I craved was at a house not far away.

I asked if he remembered the evening with Mrs Duvane and her nephew. He stood still and I halted beside him. 'Duvane?' he said, as if he were trying to recall the name, but I had the sense that he remembered very well and was playing for time. I elaborated, reminding him how he had especially wanted me to come to London.

After a silence, while the smoke of his cigar drifted across my nostrils, he said, 'What made you think of her?'

I said I understood that Mrs Duvane was dead.

'Yes. She died a short while ago.' He spoke abruptly. 'How did you know?'

I said, perhaps without enough thought, 'Toby heard something. At the Leightons'—'

'*Toby?* What have the Duvanes to do with him?'

He was facing me now and I could recognise his anger, though his face was unclear in the dusk. I said, 'He heard Mr Leighton talking about them. After dinner.'

'And then?' His voice had a roughness, like a scraped match.

Less certain now I said, 'Toby overheard Guy's father mention your name. He said – he said he wouldn't like to be in your shoes.'

'He said *what*?'

'Well, that's what he heard. And – as you can imagine – I wondered what it meant.'

'It meant nothing at all. Some damn bit of after-dinner gossip – too much port and not enough sense. And what in God's name was Toby doing, listening at keyholes?'

'He wasn't—'

'And for that matter, repeating what he'd heard? Damn the boy!'

I could feel my own anger rising. 'He was troubled. He's not a grown man – he knows nothing about finances or the law—'

'More's the pity. But I'm damned if I can see why he has to pick up sordid pieces of gossip and produce them like trophies when he gets home. Why in God's name should he trouble you?'

'Who else should he come to? He's always talked of things that worried him.'

'Gossip about his father is something which I think he could well keep to himself. Scurrilous unfounded gossip. If he had any questions, why didn't he come to me?'

I tried to think of words that might not wound him. 'You are not, in these days, very close. He's a little afraid of you – surely you can see that?'

Alexander drew on his cigar. 'Afraid ... well, I daresay. A little fear does no harm. I was afraid of my own father.'

'It doesn't encourage a boy to talk.'

He shrugged this away. 'I must speak to him.'

'Please don't!'

'My dear Isabel, this is my business. If my son repeats unfounded gossip, I've every right to rebuke him.'

I walked in silence. The garden was quite dark now – just the glow of his cigar and lamplight from the windows of the house. I said, almost to myself, 'Unfounded?'

'What d'you mean?' Again a rasp in his voice.

'I simply wondered. They were strange words.'

'Men say a lot of strange things when they've dined well. If

116

Toby'd had more sense, he'd have paid no attention to them.'

I didn't reply. Disturbing memories were coming into my mind, but it was late, and I had no heart or energy to pursue them. Something of Alexander's power kept me silent; for this moment, despite my uncertainties, he was in command.

Toby was late returning that night. Alexander was restless, briefly scanning his newspaper, then rising from his chair to pull back the curtain and look from the window. His unease disturbed me and at last I said that I was going to bed.

'Very well, very well.' His voice was dismissive. I lay in bed, wakeful. For a time the house was quiet, except for the fringe noise of the sea. Then I heard the pony trap and the sound of Toby's return. I could hear Alexander's voice, and Toby's in answer. Then I heard a door close.

After a time I slept. I had not heard either Toby or Alexander come up to bed.

August 18th

I dressed hurriedly the next morning. The sky was grey, a wind riding in from the shore: I could see the shrubs and trees bending with it. At the breakfast table I found Alexander and Toby eating in silence. As I sat down Alexander made a grunt of acknowledgement, and Toby gave me a wan smile. Alexander finished his coffee, put his cup down with a small decisive sound and rose to his feet. 'I've work to do,' he said. Toby kept his eyes on the table. When the door closed, he seemed to relax, as if he could breathe more easily.

I said, 'Your father talked to you last night?'

He made a grimace. 'He certainly did. I got the whole works.'

'What did he say?'

'Oh ... you can imagine. How I shouldn't listen to gossip, much less repeat it. He was ... well, I think he was angrier than he need've been.'

This pressed on a nerve of apprehension, for I could under-stand precisely what Toby meant. I said, 'I'm sorry I spoke of it to Alexander. But the words troubled me.'

'Well, they were rather odd, weren't they? Father was pretty ruffled. Jumpy. It's strange, but I felt somehow sorry for him.'

117

This too went home, and I recalled Alexander when he had said of Toby, 'We used to be such friends.' In the gulf between Alexander and his son there was a tenuous thread of affection. Unease constrained us that morning, and I was glad when Guy Leighton arrived in a pony trap. He was two years older than Toby, taller, dark, hair crisply curled. His manner, I thought, was a little arrogant, though he was able to cover this with the necessary politeness when he talked to Alexander or me. How much, I wondered, did he know of the 'gossip' which Toby had repeated? Was there perhaps in his manner an element of scorn? I was glad when he spoke of the prospects for sailing.

'Risky business,' Alexander said. 'Hope you know what you're doing.'

'I think so, sir.' Guy spoke with a slight drawl. 'I've been sailing since I was six. My father taught me, and he was a hard taskmaster.'

Alexander grunted. 'You plan to go today?'

'That's the idea, sir. The weather they say is improving. And there's a good wind.'

Another grunt. 'Where's your boat?'

'Totland Bay. We plan to sail round Hatherwood Point and the Needles, back here to the bay.'

'Round the Needles, eh? Tricky waters there, I understand.'

'So I believe, sir. But if he knows what he's about, a good sailor can manage perfectly well. Only fools get into trouble.'

Toby said, 'Guy really does know about sailing, Father.'

Alexander glanced at his son with concealed impatience, but said only, 'Just as well. You have to know your bowsprit from your topsail, eh, Guy?'

'That's correct, sir.'

The two of them, Toby and Guy, went from the room, and I followed them. It was true that the sky was clearing, but the wind drove briskly.

Guy held up a wetted finger. 'That's what we need,' he said. 'It'll be the best kind of day.'

I watched them go. Toby turned to wave; I thought they looked happy together – Guy the elder, Toby, his fair hair adrift in the wind, talking eagerly. As they moved out of sight I felt a little fall of heart. Absurd, for they would be back by evening. But I didn't want to return to the house, and to Alexander.

I could, I found, as the time passed, settle to nothing. Alexander stayed mostly in his study; when he appeared he was morose and silent. I was not surprised when Beatrice came in after luncheon. It seemed appropriate that she should come on this uncomfortable day.

As always, I could not quite make out the current that ran between Beatrice and Alexander. It was as if they had recently broken off a disturbing conversation which needed further time. Almost as adults are, together, when they have a secret and a child is present. But I was not a child, and unease persisted.

Beatrice suggested a walk. The day was again sunless, the promise of clear skies had not endured, and the wind was lively. We went from the back gate on to the Down. Climbing the path, we found the wind stronger there and I glanced down to the sea. Grey, with plumes of white, the little crash as waves met the shore. Toby and Guy? I reminded myself of Guy's confidence – good sailing weather, he had said. I was not afraid for them. Or ... perhaps I told myself I was not afraid; Toby had sailed in rougher weather than this. They would be home at the end of the day, tousled, exhausted, exhilarated, full of talk, as all sportsmen are when the sport is done. For the present, Beatrice and Alexander, a little ahead of me, walked purposefully over the Down.

I heard Beatrice say my name with that thread of impatience which meant that she had spoken already and I hadn't heard.

'I'm sorry?' I said.

'I wondered what news you had of Mr Malleson? He still stays on the island, I believe.'

I said, 'Yes.'

'Surprising, perhaps, considering his beliefs – or rather, one might say, lack of them.'

I knew it would be best to contain the anger rising within me. 'He writes the truth as he sees it,' I said.

'Ha!' Alexander gave a swing of his walking stick. 'Much good does that do, when the truth as he sees it goes contrary to the basic beliefs of Christians the world over.'

Beatrice said, 'One cannot but agree. Mr Malleson has done nothing but harm by his writing. Undermining the simple belief of God-fearing people.'

119

I tried to control the anger, rising fast now. 'He has been entirely true to his own beliefs. The poet said there was more faith in honest doubt—'

'Ah! Poets,' Alexander said, dismissing them.

Beatrice was turned to me. 'Of course Mr Malleson is a friend of yours?'

I said, 'Yes. He is a friend.'

'Perhaps that's as well,' Beatrice said, 'for I cannot believe he has many friends on the island.'

My heart was beating fast; I kept my head down. It was becoming clear to me that Beatrice had suspicions – if not more – about my friendship with Piers. However, I could not help saying, 'I think he has true friends. People who believe as he does, and trust what he says.'

Beatrice lifted her chin and put a hand to the brim of her hat. 'Then I must say one can only feel sorry for them.'

'Do you mean,' I said rashly, 'that you feel sorry for me?'

Beatrice smiled, the thin smile I knew well. 'Oh, my dear Isabel, you mustn't take things so personally – must she, Alexander?'

Alexander gave a grunt of acknowledgement. I didn't think he was paying much attention to Beatrice at this moment, and I was obscurely grateful for that. We all walked on in silence. I knew – as I had known for some time – that Beatrice was an enemy. But I felt that something constrained her, prevented her from openly confronting me, or speaking directly to Alexander of her suspicions (if she had them) of Piers and myself.

As we came to the highest point of the Down, we paused, as if someone had spoken to us. The wind bullied us with new strength. The sea showed the forming of white on a grey-green dissolving surface. The whip of the wind and the roughened sea far down made my head spin, and I covered my face with my hands. Beatrice said, 'Are you quite well, dear?'

I shook my head to clear it of confusion. Alexander was looking at me with a mixture of concern and impatience. I said, yes, I was all right. But I knew that the day had turned rough and angry, not only in sea and sky, but within me as well. I was all right, I said untruthfully, but I would rather go no further.

As we turned into the full force of the wind, a small smudge of white out there on the sea caught my eye. It was not dissolving as were the white plumes of water; it kept its shape, as it plunged and lifted with the swell of the sea. The craft looked very small, and of course I could not tell who sailed in her, but I stood still, staring out into the grey salty distance, watching the movement there.

August 25th
Perhaps it is better to write this down, as I have written everything else.

I must go back to that moment on the cliff top. Alexander and Beatrice stood on either side of me, as if I had commanded them to. I could not take my eyes from that frail wing of sail, at the mercy of the sea.

'Toby—' I said, but Alexander cut in sharply.

'He'd never be out there in this weather. At least his friend Guy would have more sense.'

Fear gripped my stomach, and at first I didn't reply. Beatrice echoed Alexander: young though they were, Guy and Toby were experienced sailors, not foolhardy...

'*Some*one is in danger,' I said. My throat was dry; a little rain stung my cheek. Though I was the smallest of the three, I went ahead of them, hurrying down the cliff path. I heard Alexander call to me, words stripped away on the wind. After some moments he came close to me. 'Isabel! Take care – you're going too fast!'

I paid no attention, but now, with his long stride, he was keeping pace with me. 'We'll gain nothing by falling down the cliff face. And we don't know whose craft that is.'

I scarcely slowed my step. 'I have to find out. I'm afraid.'

'But what can we do?'

Indeed, I had small idea. I knew well where the nearest lifeboat was – at Brook, where I had seen (how long ago?) the launch of the boat and the rescue. And would the coastguards have seen this small craft? There would be fishermen on the shore of the bay, but would they set out in this angry sea? I had to reach the bay. Beatrice lagged a little way behind. I had almost forgotten her, but I saw as she drew near that her mouth was set and her eyes watered. And I remembered that of my children it was Toby for whom she cared most.

We reached the shore. With Alexander, I stumbled over the shingle, the sea loud in my ears. A fisherman crouched by his boat, surveying the strong advance and plunge of the grey sea.

I shouted to him, above the wind. I pointed to the wing of sail, shouting that the craft was in danger – that something must be done. He shrugged and shook his head. I turned in desperation to Alexander, but he said only, his voice rough in the wind, 'What can the man do? Drown himself?'

The fisherman waved one arm. 'Lifeboat's over at Brook. Coastguards'll have seen her, no doubt. But the water's dangerous there – flood tide and a storm-force wind.'

I stood there on the windblown shore. The sea drove towards us as if in anger. Though it was only afternoon, the sky seemed to flood with evening. Alexander was trying to make me move, saying that we could do no good here, but I shook my head. I had no doubt now that Toby and Guy were in that buffeted craft out there, and I could not move. Again Alexander said that we must take shelter, but before I could answer him, I heard the maroon gun. A great sound, louder than the wind and the sea. By now there was a small crowd on the shore and all heads turned. 'They've seen her,' the fisherman said. 'They'll be gathering, going out down the slipway.'

There was heavier rain on the wind now. Both Alexander and Beatrice were speaking to me, words I could make no sense of, except that Alexander pulled at my arm, as if to draw me to shelter. But still I could not move. My eyes strained towards the salt-misty distance where I could just perceive the red iron-stone cliffs below Brook, from where the lifeboat would come. How vividly in my mind's eye could I see the lifeboat and the men in their shining oilskins and lifebelts. The fisherman beside me was standing now and I was aware of the small but growing crowd of people on the windy shore. I heard their voices, rising as the lifeboat came into sight, plunging through the waves – '*There she is*!' I was lost to them all now, tethered to the lifeboat travelling so surely to rescue ... Rescue? The small wing of sail was now almost lost to sight. I heard a man's voice nearby – 'Too strong a wind for a craft like that. Looks like they've capsized – running before the wind. Flood the sail then. Strong currents out there – worst of the island.' Still I could not move. I began to shiver with a kind of cold fever. The wind drove harder; I could feel the wet and the cold searching my clothes, reaching my skin. Alexander's voice was loud in protest but I still resisted him. I had to stay here to the end. Whatever the end might be.

Voices about us came louder now, and I could see that the lifeboat had found its quarry. I could not define the words – wind, cold and fear dulled my hearing. But I caught a note of excitement – perhaps hope? No, nothing could move me from this place, if there was hope.

Indeed, I had still at that time, I think, standing there, a little hope. There was movement out to sea, the plunge of the lifeboat; formless voices, shrill in the wind, men moving here on the shore towards the travelling waves; all these seemed to suggest life. I clasped my arms round my body to quiet its shivering. They were coming in, the men in their streaming lifejackets pulling on the oars. Nearer. Nearer. I felt the forward surge of the crowd, but I was held, frozen, immobile. The lifeboat was coming in and voices about me seemed to grow louder; men's voices now, rough with exertion and fatigue. Alexander went forward and, standing there, still without moving, I held on to the last of my hope.

Then it seemed to me that all the voices fell silent, and I could only hear the sea and the wind, and the cry of the gulls, storm-blown. (How I had loved the sea, and now it was an enemy.) I saw that the men in the lifeboat were bending over their craft, and what it contained. I did move forward a little then, but Alexander strode quickly towards me, his face without colour, dashed with wind and spray.

'No,' he said. 'No.'

I looked at him with wordless pleading. 'Toby?'

He gave a sharp jerk of his head. 'Yes. Both of them – Guy too. The men have done all they could.'

I did not move. There seemed to come from the crowd, a sigh, barely audible above the wind. An impulse went through me to cry out, but I made no sound. Much activity now, of the lifeboatmen, drenched and stern-faced after the failed rescue, of the helpers on the shore, murmuring, lamentation. I do not know how long I stood there in the cold sea wind. 'Come now, my dear,' Alexander was saying, and Beatrice echoed him. 'You must come home. You're soaked through. You'll be ill.'

But still I stood there, for it seemed necessary to stay in this place, as if there were some duty to be performed here.

How great a crowd there seemed to be now on the familiar shore. I thought they were all strangers. Someone (Beatrice, perhaps?) had put a heavy coat over my shoulders. I covered my face with my hands, for the rain drove with increasing strength. Then I turned and began to walk away.

Chapter 14
Kate and Perdita – 1940

'Section Commander Lewis?' The voice on the telephone was feminine, young, impersonal. Kate said yes, and waited. 'Senior Commander Spalding would like to speak to you.'

Thought she might, Kate said to herself, playing with a pencil on her desk. Isabel's journal was open before her and the wash of that angry sea still sounded in her ears.

'I have your letter, Lewis.'

'Yes, ma'am. Good,' she added, without much conviction.

'I'm sure you realise that overstaying your leave is a serious offence. We shall have to deal with the consequences when you return.'

'Yes, ma'am. I understand that. But I do need to ask for an extension – for the ashes.'

'The ashes?'

'Of my grandmother.' Sounds like a foreign phrase book, Kate thought. 'Of my grandmother,' she repeated, and saw again the figure on the cold shore, wrapping herself against the wind, and that final loss. 'She wanted them scattered on the island. Where she lived. I promised her I'd do that.'

'Ah.' A brief recognition, perhaps of mortality. 'However, I've never really felt, Lewis, that you fully grasp the necessity for obedience.'

'I'm sorry, ma'am. I do try.'

'When is this ceremony to take place?'

'In a few days. My cousin has to get back from Cumberland. We're going together. Then it'll all be over.'

'Yes, indeed. Very well – but after this ceremony, you will return here to HQ.'

'Yes, ma'am. Thank you.'

Kate put down the telephone. The present had uncomfortably intruded on the vivid and absorbing past. A return to HQ in the barricaded South Coast town – and then? The question still pursued her and needed soon to be answered. Idly, she turned back the pages of Isabel's journal. Back past the cold sojourn on the shore, watching the lifeboat come in. Back to the encounters with Piers Malleson, when Isabel spoke of 'that other girl, in difficult love, in a different and future time'. Kate rose from her chair, thrust a hand through her hair. Why the hell didn't I talk to her? Tell her about Charles? For she seemed to know... Know something, at any rate.

Lighting a cigarette, she remembered that last doomed summer of 1939, walking with Charles over the Down, where Isabel had walked. (And the house, Rosecroft, mysteriously available – 'let for the summer'. Free for two magical weeks – sometimes more – when she and Charles could hide away there.)

But there had been a feeling of unease at that time, she remembered – not only the threat of war, but something unspoken between them. What had been on his mind? She couldn't know, would never know now. Did that moment to come, the violent snatching from life in Coventry, cast its shadow? Or was he beginning to chafe against the duplicity, the covert meetings, times always threatened with their end?

Mysteries in the air: herself and Charles – and grandmother Isabel, going secretly to her lover's house. An old passion, lost now; yet strangely alive, as if that time of vanished summers on the shore merged with these shabby streets, the shards of broken glass, the angry stream of fire from incendiary bombs...

Hungry for more evidence of the past, Kate searched among the papers in the box. She found a photograph of Toby: yellow, faded, spotted with age. But the face so very young, wide-eyed, solemn, promising good things, as the portraits of the handsome young always do... (And the cold shore; and the lifeboat coming in.) She could find nothing of Piers Malleson – not surprisingly, perhaps.

And nothing, as far as she could see, of Jasper Vye.

She picked up his letter from her desk, where it had lain so far unanswered. *My name is Jasper Vye. I don't know if it means anything to you. But I knew your grandmother. How do I end this letter? In hope, I think.*

There is, Kate thought, a surprising thread of comfort in that cryptic letter. And as soon as Perdita returned later that afternoon she would make some reply.

Her cousin arrived just after four o'clock, with her usual air of having cheerfully survived an avalanche. 'Gosh,' she said, pulling off her woolly hat, 'all those people sheltering in the tube. You just pick your way round them and keep wanting to apologise. Women and kids, and old men...' Taking off her coat, talking as she did so, she said, 'No one prepared us for all this, did they? There was that other war – I just remember the end of it: people shouting and waving flags – I can just remember that. And my mother weeping because my father had been killed and she couldn't wave any flags. But no one told us we'd find ourselves here in the Blitz, Gerald on ops, and you...' She broke off, the young face abashed. 'Am I talking too much? Saying the wrong thing?'

Kate grinned and flung herself into a chair. 'No. I'm just bloody glad to see you. How was the boy?'

'Oh ... up and eating. There wasn't much wrong: like I said, it was Bronwen's way of telling me where "my duty lay". No, maybe that's mean. There she is, up there with the children, thinking every night about Gerald. And she's glad to have me there, because I'm so damned optimistic, I don't know why. I keep telling her he'll be all right, and I think she half believes me...' She waved a hand at the journals. 'Have you read more?'

'A whole lot more,' Kate said, showing Perdita the photograph of Toby and telling her the story.

Perdita looked at the photograph with absorbed interest. 'She must have remembered him every day of her life. Rebecca too. But she never talked of them. They were just names.'

'We didn't ask,' Kate said again. 'But how much did *she* know? One hell of a lot, it seems to me.'

Perdita nodded. 'Almost as if she were here in the room with us – a bit like that, isn't it? And this letter.'

'From Jasper Vye. Here...' She handed it to Perdita, who scanned it, then said, 'It's odd, isn't it? Kind of magic, as if something in the journals had come alive. Let's ring him *now*.'

As Kate lifted the telephone she heard the first wail of the siren: Perdita was sitting with alert attention.

A voice at the other end of the line: 'Jasper Vye here.' She felt a small twinge of triumph and explained herself. His voice was not unpleasing, dry, perhaps ironic. At least, interested.

Yes, he would come. He would be busy during the day, but free in the evening. He would come by tube, and be at Kate's flat about half-past-seven. He gave these small bits of information as one who takes an orderly view of life, in spite of wartime disruptions. 'Goodbye,' he said on an upward note, as if in amused expectation.

Kate put down the receiver. 'Why do I feel I've achieved something? Excited? I haven't felt excited about anything since Charles died.'

Perdita said it was because of Isabel, because he was there at that time. The island time.

Chapter 15
Isabel – 1900

September

I am still on the island. And this morning I began to write again. At first I had no energy to lift the book or my pen.

Since we were so well known in Freshwater – indeed in other parts of the island – there were many messages of condolence, flowers, other tokens of sympathy. I received these with all the grace I could muster, but in truth I saw them as if through a pane of glass. They did not – could not, I am afraid – touch my heart. I was somewhat ashamed of this, for I saw the tears in their eyes – both men and women – and knew they grieved for me. It was surely lacking in true feeling, or at any rate in some way discourteous, not to respond, offering the chance for a kiss, even a heartfelt embrace.

But I cannot give them that. I must surely disappoint them, and for this I am sorry. Perhaps a time will come when I will behave as it would seem a grieving mother should behave. But that time is not yet.

Strangely it is Alexander who (if I may so put it) does best at this. Alexander, it seems, has reverted to the father who took pride in and cherished his son. He has perhaps forgotten, or lost in the torment of grief, the later years when Toby had grown distant from him. Alexander, who has always seemed to look on shows of emotion as somewhat beneath him, even deserving of contempt, finds that the tears spill when friends offer comfort, his handkerchief is ever at his face...

I write, I see, not in true sympathy: with an edge, even, of anger. Yes, I cannot deny it: something in Alexander's outward grief touches a nerve within me, and I want to cry out, *Have*

129

you forgotten? Do you remember how you last spoke to him, of him?

But then the anger fades and I reach a kind of blank reason. Is it not because he is aware of failure, of some lack of love, that he now weeps for the son he cannot make reparation to, who has left him for ever? And indeed, from my place of dry mourning, I am aware of something else about Alexander's expressions of grief – they are somewhat extreme, out of control. This gives me a sensation of disquiet, and I trace this back to the day of Toby's funeral.

The day was grey, warm with a quiet sullen sea. You might even say the weather mourned. I walked with Alexander, my arm in his. We did not often touch now, but at this moment I had the sensation that he needed my support. Did we need each other? Perhaps there was an inevitable bond: together we had given this life, and together we had seen it go.

Both Marigold and Sylvia had come to the island. Something in me doubted the wisdom of this, but I could not have prevented them. Sylvia was crying audibly, making heads turn. Marigold, stern-faced (I suddenly saw her as a woman, with her own troubled life) was trying to hush her.

The parson who took the service was but little known to me: I listened to him, and to the familiar words, but they didn't seem to have anything to do with Toby. Toby was a young man, running off to go sailing, his face alight with expectation and enjoyment. He was not here, amongst the formal flags of desolation, the words of Scripture, beautiful though they were. (I had, as we walked into the church, caught a glimpse of Piers, sitting alone. Briefly our eyes met; I could read nothing in his face.)

The service was coming to an end. I had then a moment's panic, as if the true agony of parting shot through the words and the obligatory hymns, and I wanted to cry out and stop them all, protest that Toby was not dead, not there, he was off somewhere in the delight of being young.

But this moment passed, for I made a great effort, and the church and the company were again unreal, to do with someone else, not Toby. Even at the graveside, I didn't weep. I felt only the angular pain in my chest, like the teeth of an animal, and the hot pressure behind my eyes that did not result in tears.

It was as we turned away from the grave that I caught the sudden flash of recognition. I thought for a moment that my mind was adrift and I was imagining familiarity where there was none. A face turned to me, wearing a look of indecision – to make acknowledgement or not? The face of a young man, known, seen by me at some time.

I couldn't put him into context, but the familiarity troubled me. I looked back once again before I stepped into the carriage. A dark-haired, young man's face... Suddenly in the midst of this strange unmerciful day I had a moment of recognition: I had seen him talking to Alexander on an island road, and Alexander had given me his name. An unusual name ... Jasper. Jasper Vye.

With the memory of the name, I turned sharply to look at Alexander, for surely he had noticed the face which was known to him? But his head was down, his face set; I couldn't know if he had seen the young man called Jasper or not. Perhaps he was still enfolded in his grief, his eyes unfocused with tears. Yet I was aware of a rigidity in his body, as if he were not quite unaware.

September 6th

I do not have a clear memory of the next few days. Perhaps there is a kind of mercy in extreme occasions, a sort of numbness, as if in a crowded place full of noise and activity, one had suddenly become deaf. It is not a large mercy, but it gives one at least the sense of living outside the real world.

But I felt a touch of that world when Alexander said one evening after dinner that of course he must return to London. And when he added, 'I can only imagine that you will want to be done with this house.'

I came up from some far reverie. 'Done with...?'

'My dear Isabel, surely this place can now have only the most painful memories for you? You can't want to stay here?'

I stood in silence, looking at him. I felt quite overthrown, as if his remark had been entirely unexpected. But of course it was not so – many others would have said the same. Should I not want, after all that had happened, to turn my back on Rosecroft and the island?

But I did not. Even in this dark cavern of a world I wanted

to stay here, here in this house, from which I could hear the sea – even the sea which had taken Toby from me. And at some far point in the darkness was a threatened, even guilty light: that glimpse of Piers at the back of the church. He had written a letter which I had not put with the rest. There had been no need to conceal it – he had simply written as others had. Written from the heart, I knew that. Addressed to us both, and I could only guess at his sensation as he wrote Alexander's name.

I had not seen him alone. That was to come.

Regaining my voice I said, 'I don't want to leave the house. I belong here. Toby belonged here. Rebecca too. I ... need to stay.'

'Alone?' Alexander said.

'I've spent much time alone.'

'Your own choice, my dear. But now, with this tragedy – I would have thought... For myself...' I noticed, with a detachment that I was ashamed of, that his eyes had washed over with tears. 'For myself, I couldn't stay.' He looked over the room. 'I don't think I ever want to see this place again.'

I could feel my hands trembling; his words disturbed me at some level which I could not quite understand. I tried to say, stammering a little, that in time, surely, his feelings would soften, would change.

He didn't answer me at first. He dashed one hand across his eyes, but I thought his mind was active now, coming clear of grief. 'There is just one thing – I have to consider my financial position.'

For this I was entirely unprepared. I said, 'But how has that changed? The house is ours now. We – I – don't live lavishly here.'

His face was grave, preoccupied, his tears dried. 'I have never discussed financial questions with you. It is a man's task to provide for his children and his home.'

I acknowledged that this he had always done. But, I added, there was the legacy that had come to me from my parents.

He gave a brief nod. 'I have always looked on that as your own. But it might be that we shall have to make use of it.'

It was as he spoke that the memory came back to me. I had (perhaps unconsciously) smothered it, because it had concerned the last words that Alexander had exchanged with Toby. I said, 'The money is for the family and their future. But I think you owe me some explanation—'

He turned to me in sudden anger. 'I have nothing to explain! I am simply telling you that my finances are not as healthy as they once were. You really don't, my dear Isabel, wish to hear details just now of the Stock Market.'

I was briefly silent. I had the sensation of a dangerous moment, of my foot on a slippery step. Then I said without further thought, 'Who *was* Gilbert Duvane?'

He turned to me, his face flushed. 'What the hell d'you mean?'

'I remember what Toby said —'

'Idle gossip, as I told you. Toby has gone: at least we can cover ill-considered words, as we have covered his grave.'

I tried to control my trembling. 'Toby spoke the truth. He must have done. He was my son, and whatever he said was – was important.' I didn't want to weep, but the tears choked my voice. 'I remember Gilbert Duvane and his aunt. I remember that evening—'

'I'll not hear any more of this! To bring this nonsense up now – *now* of all times, when ... when...'

I saw that he was indeed overcome, and I was torn between pity and anger. But before I could speak he recovered himself and said, 'I have had enough. I leave for London tonight. I think it best if you don't accompany me.'

I was left standing in the room. I should be alone here, but that was of no consequence. Indeed, I should be glad of it. Toby's voice would echo through the rooms, and this would pierce my heart, as would his childhood books with the awkward writing of his name. But I could, I thought, endure even this.

For alone, there in the familiar room, I had some sense of far comfort. It was as distant as the echo of music when the instrument is silent. Yet it held me as I stood there, my head turned a little, as if listening. I was not quite alone. She was there, the girl, formless, featureless, yet close by, speaking words of reassurance; the girl whose life I cared for, whose life I could understand.

September 15th

Warmth has returned with these last days of summer. Briefly those loaded skies have passed, and the tide comes in, lazy and sunlit, caressing the shore.

Alexander has returned to London; that is best. He grieves for Toby, but it is not my grief; we are too far from each other to offer comfort. I do not, at this time, ponder the questions about him. He holds secrets obscure to me. (Shall I know them? Perhaps ... but not yet.)

For the present I wander often by the shore, sometimes in the early morning, when it is empty except perhaps for a fisherboy. I wander slowly, held in mystery. For was it not strange that I could walk here by this sea which had taken Toby from me? I was puzzled, aware of some force that drove me, kept me upright, not quite defeated.

No, I say quickly, I am not subscribing to a creed: I am with Piers in his country of doubt. I cannot give myself to that distant and arbitrary God who scatters pain and good fortune with an unaccountable hand. And yet, as I stand here, in this body that has such a short tenure of life, I am aware of being part of some long distance, past and future; aware of strength in the midst of pain. I am afraid, but I have the power, it seems, to overcome my fear; the loss of both Toby and Rebecca has put some steel into me; I have been down to the depths of some place where iron is forged...

... I have looked at these words after a space of time. They appear to me a little grandiose, as if they had been written by someone else. Yet I feel that they are not altogether untrue.

September 16th

Today I went to him. I knew that he had waited; that it was I, not he, who must choose the time. He would be thinking of me, I knew that, and his heart would be sore for me.

I had no doubt that I should find him there, at work in his study, but the house was empty – there was no answer to the bell. I turned and walked back the way I had come, then stopped still. At a distance I could see Piers, with Beatrice at his side. No need, I told myself, to feel a small frisson of disquiet: there was nothing that Beatrice could do to me... Neither of them having yet seen me, I observed her. She had

134

grown a little stout, but was still handsome. With the years, she more closely resembled Alexander. I knew that she was still, if not my enemy, not my friend.

They were coming towards me, and I resisted the urge to escape. We met at the entrance to the house: Beatrice lifted her head, and seemed to check a remark, as if she had to recall that I had been recently and savagely bereaved. Piers' face showed no expression at all, but I reflected that he was good at that when he needed to be.

Beatrice said, 'I'm glad to have seen you, Isabel. I was going to look in to say goodbye.'

'Goodbye?'

'Yes, I'm going to London tomorrow.'

I wished her a good journey. It crossed my mind that her departure followed hard on Alexander's, but I was not greatly concerned. She spoke a little longer, not quite, I thought, at her ease, then turned, bidding us both farewell. My eyes only followed her a little way.

Piers said, 'I've been waiting for you. We'd better go indoors.'

A spark rose in me. 'I'm not afraid of being seen.'

The familiar dry smile crossed his face. 'No one's afraid of anything, my dear. But I would hope I might take you in my arms, and that would be easier in the house.'

Gladly obedient, I went ahead of him. Though it was not so long since I had been in the room, the whole place was given a different perspective by the great change in my life.

As he had promised, Piers took me in his arms. It was an embrace composed more of love than hunger, but I was for some reason a little afraid of it. I drew away, smoothing my dress, and sat down. He made no protest, merely sat also, facing me, so we were like friends, talking across the space of a room.

'My heart has ached for you,' he said, and I nodded, having accepted this.

I said, 'I remember I came to you when Rebecca died. So long ago.'

'I couldn't help you. I longed to, but I couldn't.'

I looked back to that other time. I could remember our voices in that different room. I said, 'I don't think help was possible. Nor is it now. When I think about Toby it's like

135

beating my fists against a door that's bolted. But I've only one wish – apart from his life – and that was to see you.'

He made no movement, for which I was glad. But I saw the softening of his face as he said, 'I had some doubts ... that was only natural, wasn't it?'

'Doubts?'

'Whether you would have – what shall I say? – room for me. Whether your love would be the same.'

I looked at him. At last I said, 'No, not the same: simply because nothing is the same. Nor ever will be now. After the death of your child the world is a different place. And always will be.'

'But you came to me.'

I said that I could do nothing else. It was as simple as coming home.

He looked at me in silence then. I could see that he was being careful, watching his words. I was glad of this, and at the same time apprehensive.

'It's too early,' he said at last, 'to talk of the future. On the other hand...' He glanced away from me to the window and the ridge of the Down. 'Where is Alexander?'

I told him.

'And of course he's a man most stricken, I don't doubt that. So this is no time to present him with further disruption of his life.'

I glanced quickly at him, then away. The words were clear enough: I wasn't ready to pursue them. I said, 'There is something else about Alexander.'

He waited. (I was grateful for his control; I thought I had never known a man who made so few demands, who obtruded himself so little yet, at the same time, conveyed the force of his love.) I told him what I knew about Gilbert Duvane, what Toby had overheard. 'I don't know what it means,' I said. 'Alexander can't – or won't – tell me.'

'And this of course isn't the time to cross-examine him.'

'No ... but there's much that I'd like to ask. D'you know a young man called Jasper Vye?'

He frowned. 'I don't think ... no, wait a minute. Some years ago there was a woman – Leonora Vye. She was on the island for a short time. I believe she had a son.'

I told him of the two occasions I had seen Jasper Vye. Of the impression he had made on me.

'So he was at Toby's funeral?' Piers said.

'I saw him there. But he didn't speak to me. Nor – now that I come to think of it – to Alexander. Was that not strange, perhaps?'

We faced each other and I felt a shaft of perception, some small, if sinister, enlightenment. But he was not, I saw, in the mood to pursue it now. Alexander and his secrets, whatever they might be, were not his main concern. Nor was Jasper Vye. He said, 'I know it's not the time yet. I've said so. But there *is* a future – our future. And some time we shall have to talk about it.'

Briefly I nodded. His words carried power; I couldn't deny the challenge. I looked away once more to the window and the far glint of the sea. I couldn't see the future. There was this emptiness, without Toby. There were Marigold and Sylvia, and my concern for them. And Alexander? I could see him as he was now, shadowed, angry: separated from me, in the London house...

And then there was this love. Oh yes; a love, I thought, glancing at Piers' face and away again. Just now it was muted by Toby's loss, but it was there, waiting to take command again, I had no doubt of that.

So, the future?

I had no answer for him then.

Of the steps which led to what I must call the savage recognition, it is best to write now, while I am still on the island, where – in spite of violent change – much remains the same. Where the shape of the Arch rock stands there, assaulted by the seas. (It's strange, but sometimes I see another rock there, beside the Arch. I have said absently, 'There are two tall rocks, separated from the land.' But my companion looks at me with puzzled enquiry and says something like, 'What d'you mean, two rocks?' and I recall myself, looking to the familiar single shape and say, 'No ... no, of course, there is only one.')

I am here in limbo, as it were, between the loss of Toby and the savage time that came after.

The quieter things first: a letter from Marigold, in Paris. A sadness that, after the miscarriage she had failed to conceive. 'I don't see why one can't be happy,' she wrote. 'There doesn't seem much point in life if you're not enjoying yourself.' I gave a wry smile on reading this, for it left so large a distance between her philosophy and mine that I felt at a loss. And yet there was a poignance in this distance: Marigold had been that child on the shore who had shown kindness to her younger sister, who had watched Toby's first stumbling steps. Who had fled from home, glad, it seemed, to be gone. I had felt some guilt about this, for though I loved her as I loved all my children, my greatest love had been for Toby and Rebecca, and I could not know how much she had been aware of this. Was it partly why she had rushed into a marriage which, to say the least, seemed unsuitable?

But Marigold, I thought suddenly, would have her child. With the letter in my hand, I had a great certainty of this. For a moment I felt a flood of happiness, something which was at that time indeed strange to me, as if the conception and birth were already accomplished, and I could greet my first grandchild – that particular affirmation of life, which gives its answer to death.

The sensation faded, and I was left with the letter in my hand. There was no letter from Sylvia, but I had learned not to expect one. Sylvia, from her lodgings in Bloomsbury, would leave long periods of silence, then write in a sprawling hand pages of almost indecipherable lament, mingled with an occasional upsurge of excitement when she described some peak of enjoyment... What would become of her? I had a great longing to protect her, but perhaps the time for that was past. Perhaps she too felt that my strongest love went to Toby and Rebecca. When it came to children, I thought, you have this dangerous power and this love, and before you are aware of it, you have spoken or acted wrongly and somehow damaged what you greatly care for.

And yet, as I thought about Sylvia, I had again that unexplained sensation of happiness, of some unlooked-for good that might attend her... There was no reason why Sylvia should not marry and have children: she was a pretty girl, and there would be men surely at the art school who would find nothing strange in her uncertain temperament...

138

I stood, again flooded with the mysterious consolation, the unlooked-for happiness. Perhaps, I thought, life has mercy when you least expect it: perhaps the waters of sorrow withdraw and you find yourself on a shore of sunlit warmth and calm, exhausted, stretched out like a castaway in grateful ease, the struggle done?

I put Marigold's letter aside, and with it the too easy solution of such final serenity. Marigold and Sylvia would always trouble me; and I myself was at a turning point. Bereft of Toby, estranged from Alexander, close to – and yet far from – Piers. It was possible to close one's eyes, to say there is no answer, except to stay as you are, wife – in name at least – to Alexander. Go on simply as before, living out a life, with grief behind one, as a great many people did, driving over the rough road to the inevitable but seldom-talked-of end. Without Piers.

But that left a great emptiness, a sense of time wasted, of love denied. No, I had no answer. Not yet. But I was aware of some great impending change, as if the loss of Toby had opened a gate that would swing wide and let me through into new places.

And it was in such a mood that I greeted the next day, when the other letter came.

September 26th

The morning was warm but overcast; the sea coming in with little sound but with a surly swell as if it contained the threat of storm. I saw a lone man emerge from one of the bathing machines and heard the muted splash as he gave himself to the water.

I dressed with hurried abstraction, impatient with the necessity of doing these things. Some urgency pressed on me and I went quickly downstairs to my desk in the living room. I could hear movement in the house, the usual sounds of cleaning and voices.

And then the letter.

Molly, the new parlourmaid, brought it to me. She was very young – no more than sixteen, the same age as Toby. She was shy and nervous and, fleetingly, I felt sorry for her. But I just said, 'Thank you, Molly; that'll be all.' She made an awkward diving movement, and left me.

139

I looked at the letter, as one does when the handwriting is unfamiliar, rather as if one had found a stranger in one's living room. I opened it and read:

Dear Mrs St Clair,

There is much that you do not know. Perhaps it would be better if you made a visit to London instead of staying in your own world on the island. Perhaps you will pay no attention to this letter, but I think that would be a mistake. What I write is important, I think I mean urgent. There is a date, the 30th of September. If possible, I would advise you to go then. Early. In the morning. I repeat, this is important.

The letter was unsigned. The handwriting was large but not entirely uneducated: the envelope had a smudge in one corner and no stamp: it had been delivered by hand. I put it down, as if the touch was somehow offensive. But it disturbed me, and reluctantly I picked it up again. *I think I mean urgent.* Uncomfortable words; I could not ignore them.

I didn't make a decision at once. Or rather, I made the only decision I was able to: I went to Piers' house and showed him the letter. When he had read it, I said as if it needed only this to make up my mind, 'I have to go.' I saw his reservation, and persisted, 'I simply have to go. How can I ignore it?'

He brooded, then made a gesture to the unsigned message. 'In my opinion, such letters should always be ignored. Maybe just a kind of mischief—'

'But you know what Toby told me. The man who said he wouldn't like to be in Alexander's shoes. What did *that* mean?'

'You think this letter is some kind of an answer?'

I gave a bewildered shake of my head. 'I have to find out – I have to.'

Again he brooded. 'I still want to say don't go. Probably because I feel safer when you're here on the island. We belong together here. When you go back to London, I'm afraid.'

He had not said so much in exact words before. I protested that there was nothing for him to fear, and saw at once that he recognised an easy falsehood. I repeated, colouring a little, that he had nothing to fear if he thought he would lose my love.

He looked at me levelly for some moments, then said at last, 'No – I believe all you've said is true. But words aren't enough. There's a life to be lived out, time to be spent together – or apart.'

I shivered a little; the words carried a cold threat, they underlined my fear. I stayed silent.

He went on, 'Yes, well – it may still be too soon to make decisions. But if you're going to London – that makes a difference: you can see it does.'

I said, 'I have to know the truth about Alexander.'

'And when you *do* know?'

'I can't think beyond that. Not yet. Please don't be angry.'

'Dear God, I'm not *angry*. There's nothing simple about any of this – how can there be? Least of all for you. But some time we have to face it. Oh ... don't look so distressed.' He took me in his arms, and I held him, finding a kind of desolate comfort in his embrace. As he released me he said again, 'Sometime. We love each other. And there is only this one life.'

A flood of longing and regret ran through me. 'Yes,' I said, my head down. 'Sometime. But first – I have to know. You must forgive me. My dearest – please forgive me.'

He looked at me as if I'd said something to wound him. He said. 'You know I'd forgive you anything, except denying me, denying that you love me.'

I put my arms round him and held him as if the strength of his body were a raft of life in an uncertain sea. I muttered, 'I shall always love you; whatever happens, please remember that.' At last I pulled myself from him, glanced once into his face, was afraid of what I read there, and said that I had to go. I went quickly from the house, shaken and afraid. To my anger and shame, the tears ran, as if this were another loss, like death.

September 30th

I left the island with a still heavy heart and watched the slow diminishing shape of Tennyson Down (as it was now called) and the wake of the ferry as if they divided me from life.

When I reached London I met the full force of fact. I had come here without Alexander's knowledge, simply on the strength of a letter from an unknown correspondent. Such a letter as Piers had said should be ignored... The knowledge seemed to enter my lungs like a draught of cold air. What was I doing here at the busy station, the island left behind? And for no better reason than someone unknown to me on the island had summoned me?

I recovered myself. No, that was not quite true. The letter had uncovered a depth of misgivings, the years of questions unanswered. I had the sense of one who pushes the last unlocked door into a secret place. I watched the London streets go past the windows of the hansom cab, the sound of the horse's hooves beating a corresponding sound to my heart.

The London house, when I reached it, cast its usual shadow. I looked back once at the horse cab as it clopped away down the street, then I pulled the bell. The ordinary day went on behind me. Then the door was opened by the parlourmaid called Nell, who looked startled, but I did my best to reassure her that this was a perfectly ordinary occurrence, which of course it was not. I stood there in the hall, removing my hat and scarf. I had heard voices – male and female – but with my arrival these abruptly ceased.

It was Beatrice who came into the hall. She faced me for a moment with total surprise mixed with antagonism. Even dismay. She said at last, 'We were not expecting you.'

This did not need saying, but I could see that she was beyond thinking further than the nearest cliché. I made some remark of equal ineptitude and, removing my coat, turned towards the living room.

Beatrice then made an exclamation and put out a hand as if she would prevent me, but this was my house and I was going to do as I pleased. As I had determined to do (it now became clear to me) from the beginning.

Once in the room, I paused. Of course it was Alexander I saw first. He was standing by the mantelpiece and his expression as he saw me was composed of astonishment, anger and, I thought, fear. 'Isabel! What in God's name are you doing here?'

I felt a rising anger, meeting his own. 'This is my house as well as yours, Alexander. I came because I believe something is wrong.'

I let my glance go to the other two people in the room. Other than Beatrice, that was. A man and a woman. It was the woman who first arrested my attention. She was dark, no longer young, but with fine eyes in a face that was used to admiration and command. But she was now, I thought, hiding behind a mask of confidence, apprehensive. Beatrice had spoken her name: Mrs Leonora Vye. She gave a small nod of her head, while I sought for the moment when I had seen her before.

Not finding it, I turned to the man who was young, though not in his first youth. He was also familiar, for I knew him from that chance meeting on the island when he had been speaking to Alexander. And again at Toby's funeral. 'Her son, Jasper Vye,' Beatrice said. He came forward and took my hand. Something in his face touched a chord within me, as if at some distant time I had known him well. But that could not have been so. He said, 'Mrs St Clair, I have to give you my condolences on the death of your son.'

I acknowledged this, for it was sincerely said. But it was not what I had come to hear.

He went on, 'Perhaps we should all sit down,' and I reflected that this young man of familiar aspect was, of all of us, most in control. In spite of Beatrice and Alexander. In spite of his mother, who was looking at me with penetrating curiosity.

Alexander had grown a little pale, but he spoke with (almost) his usual authority when he said to Jasper's mother, 'I think, as my wife has come so unexpectedly, it would be best if you and Jasper left us now.'

I saw uncertainty on her face, but Jasper said, 'D'you really think so, sir?'

Alexander looked at him with thwarted anger. Jasper went on, 'I don't have to remind you what Gilbert Duvane has threatened to do.'

The name pricked my attention and I looked with enquiry at Jasper, and then at Beatrice, who muttered, 'He threatens to cause trouble.'

'Damn him,' Alexander said, 'he has nothing to go on. Isabel – none of this is to do with you.'

'On the contrary, Alexander, it has everything to do with me. I remember Gilbert Duvane. I remember too what Toby told me only a short time ago. What he overheard.'

There was a brief silence. The discomfort in the room was palpable. I said, 'What does Gilbert Duvane threaten to do?'

Alexander, sitting now, put his head down with a jutting movement, hands clasped between his knees. 'He threatens to expose me.'

I said, 'What is there to expose?'

A deeper silence. Then, 'Nothing. Nothing. Or nothing he can prove.'

I said, 'I don't fully understand that.'

'There's no reason why you should, Isabel.'

'But I think there's every reason,' I said again. I looked round at Beatrice, Leonora Vye, and her son, Jasper. 'I have to ask what Mrs Vye and her son are doing here. If there's trouble, it's my place to know about it.'

Leonora lifted her chin, as if in challenge, and it was at that moment that, through the mists of the past, I believed I could recall when I had seen her before ... A brief moment, long past, but scarred into my memory, for she had stood there on the shore, regarding me and the children with something near antagonism. So vivid had she been that I had often dreamed of her.

I looked at her with recognition and she faced me with something of the same scornful pity which she had shown so long ago. But it was Jasper who spoke. Jasper Vye, it seemed to me, formed a point of benign sanity in the uncomfortable atmosphere of the room.

'That's of course true, Mrs St Clair. But I think it best if your husband speaks first—'

'My God, I'll speak when I want to.' I knew that note in Alexander's voice of extreme exasperation, outrage that anyone should try to usurp his place of command. He went on more quietly, 'Gilbert Duvane feels that he has been deprived of money that his late aunt invested with me. The money was invested in shares whose value has, I regret to say, fallen. The interest remains. Mrs Duvane received it for the last years of her life. When she died, the interest went to her nephew. He had no reason to be anything less than content. However he is getting married – rather late in life. He wishes to realise some capital, and I have had to ask him to give me time.'

'Time?' I said.

He gave me a look of exasperation. 'I don't expect you to understand, Isabel. We've never discussed matters of my legal business.'

'Perhaps it would have been better, sir, if you had.'

I looked at Jasper Vye with speculation. Some long arithmetic of uncertainty, of latent wondering, was coming to shape in my mind.

Alexander said, 'I must ask you, Jasper, to leave this house.'

'And I?' Jasper's mother spoke. 'Am I to be turned out too?'

Alexander looked at her with an expression that I could not read, and said at last, 'I am not "turning you out", Leonora. But now that my wife is here, I am asking you to leave. With your son.'

I could hear Beatrice give a small intake of breath. Beatrice, it occurred to me, was the least comfortable person in this room of people in varying stages of discomfort. After a moment of indecision, Leonora Vye wrapped her scarf more firmly about her and made for the door. I watched her with deep fascination: I both wanted and did not want her to go. She turned in the doorway. 'Are you coming, Jasper?'

'If you'll forgive me, Mother, I prefer to stay.'

She turned with abrupt anger and left the room. Alexander paid no attention to the crisp closing of the door but said only, 'I also asked you to go, Jasper.'

Jasper stood, at ease it seemed. Or at any rate, most strangely not overwhelmed by Alexander. I looked from one to the other. A brief silence was broken by the sudden sound of weeping: Beatrice, in a chair at my side, her head in her hands.

No one made a move to comfort her, so I put a hand on her arm. Alexander said, 'Beatrice, please control yourself.'

I said, 'Alexander.' He did not look at me, but his head was lifted. 'I want the truth. All of it.'

Beatrice's weeping grew louder. I had never thought of Beatrice as one who wept: all of this time was strange. Jasper Vye said, almost absently, 'I'm afraid it won't be a happy truth.'

I gave him a brief accepting glance, for I could not of course expect it to be happy. In a strangled voice, Beatrice said, 'There was no need for you to come here, Isabel, no need for you to know anything—'

145

'There is every need! I am Alexander's wife still. I have borne his children, and only a little while ago my beloved son was lost...'

'*Our* son, Isabel,' Alexander muttered.

'Yes ... yes, our son. But I have had enough of being kept in the dark. Yes, I can understand that I have shut myself away because I so loved the island. So loved ...' I broke off, for I must not now dwell on what else I loved there. 'But I want everything given to me now.'

So I said, but even as I spoke I felt a little fall of courage. It was easier to cry passionately for the truth than truly to desire it. I held my hands together to control their trembling. 'When you say Gilbert Duvane cannot *prove* anything – what does that mean?'

The sound of Beatrice's weeping had quietened. Alexander looked tired; I thought some of his anger had run out of him.

'It was necessary for me to raise money – no, Isabel, let me speak. You asked for the truth: then listen to it. Beatrice, please keep quiet. Sums of money are entrusted to me – yes, entrusted is the word for investment. It became necessary for me to – let's say, find resources – more than I possessed. I was able, in my position of trust, to use the capital to my advantage... Beatrice, if you don't control yourself I shall have to ask you to leave the room.'

I said, 'Your position of trust ... which, as I understand it, you have abused?'

Alexander's face took on even more deeply the lines of tiredness. 'Yes,' he said, 'that is true. But none of my clients has suffered. The interest due to them has been paid. Faithfully paid—'

'Faithfully?' I said.

'You speak with irony, my dear Isabel. It was as faithful as I could make it. So long as the clients made no enquiries about their original capital, they had no cause to complain.'

I said, 'I don't fully understand the matter, of course. But the outline of what you're saying seems clear to me. In all this time – I don't know for how long, but I suspect for a long time – you have been defrauding people who trusted their money to you—'

Beatrice had risen to her feet. 'I cannot listen to this any

146

more. There was no need for you – for anyone – to know. No need ...' Handkerchief to her face, she left the room. Now there was only Alexander, Jasper Vye and myself.

'When you say defrauding,' Alexander said, 'I would like to make it plain that no one suffered. And I was able to manage the financial affairs so that those with least to spare lost least. It was no easy task. I worked hard.'

I took a breath. 'For how long?'

He looked at me, the tired lines deeply graven. 'For many years, Isabel.'

No, it was not, as Jasper Vye, had foretold, a happy truth. I glanced at Jasper as he sat there, keeping his silence. He seemed to be waiting. Unlike his mother and Beatrice, he held his ground. Briefly, I wondered why.

I said to Alexander, 'All this time, then?'

He nodded. Jasper Vye was still silent. I said simply, 'Why?'

The only sound then was the ticking of the clock. I saw a glance go between Alexander and the younger man. There was some deep communication between them which heightened the sense of waiting.

Then Jasper said, 'Perhaps it is for me to speak?'

Alexander made a convulsive movement, rising to his feet. 'No, confound it, I tell my own story.'

Jasper said, 'As you wish.'

Alexander took one or two strides about the room, then, hand on the mantelpiece, looked down on me, sitting there. He seemed at the same time to be looking at the long past, those summers on the island. But, before he spoke, realisation began to enlarge in my mind, a sudden opening.

And when Alexander said, 'I must first tell you that Jasper is my son,' I was at once surprised and accepting. Shocked, yet old with knowledge. I turned to look at him and wondered how I had ever not known, for he so greatly resembled Alexander. A gentler Alexander, but the set of the dark eyes, something in the turn of the mouth when he smiled – these were plain to read.

He was turned to me with a kind of open pity. 'Yes,' he said, 'I am his son. And my mother—'

'Is of course,' I replied, 'Leonora. The lady who has just

147

left us. And who wrote the letter I found in the book.' I turned to Alexander. 'You made little of it but, of course, that was untrue. As so much was untrue.' The long years of deception seemed to unroll in my mind. Seen from the perspective of this truth, so much made a dark sense.

'However,' Alexander said, 'any connection between Jasper's mother and myself is now over.'

'It certainly is,' Jasper said, but without rancour. 'Mother is as far from you, Father, as you are from her. I've learned a great deal. Mother and I have argued – no, I must say, quarrelled – about this. When I discovered that she had demanded more money from you than was reasonable—'

'Is it necessary for Isabel to hear this...' Alexander began.

I said, 'Entirely necessary. When, Mr Vye, you say "reasonable"...?'

'My mother, in her position of an unacknowledged "wife" with a young child, naturally needed support and she was granted that.' Jasper sounded calm, even detached. 'But without my knowing it – I was, after all, a child – she threatened my father with exposure if he didn't, let's say, substantially increase the amount he gave her.'

He paused, and I sat there, absorbing this. Threat. More money. The whole picture was coming clear. I saw Alexander with this self-imposed shadow on him.

'And,' I said, 'it became necessary to find more money – secret money.'

'Precisely,' Alexander said. His voice had an edge of exasperated anger.

'And there were times,' I said, 'when it became even necessary for you to escape – to be out of the country. When you told me we were to go to Italy...'

I saw the twitch of pain that went over his face at that remembrance. 'There was trouble brewing – or so I thought. An employee in the firm seemed to have got wind of what was going on. I dismissed him, but he threatened blackmail. I had to be out of the way...' he shrugged. 'It's useless, too late, to make any kind of apology. I've lived my life as it seemed best to me—'

'As you wanted to live it,' I said.

'If you like. Most of us do that, one way or another. You and

I were often at a distance from each other. Your love for the island, for one thing. I never felt you were happy in London.'

I agreed that this was true. 'And Leonora?' I asked.

'I first met her on the island. She was a young widow, without children. She had cousins at Freshwater and was staying with them while she tried to plan her life. Her husband had suffered from some mental instability and had committed suicide. She had little money and there were legal complications about her husband's estate. It was arranged that when she returned to London she should consult me professionally.' He shrugged again. 'She was a very attractive woman, with much strength of personality. I fell in love with her.'

My head was down. 'But,' I said, 'you didn't tell me, and end our marriage? Surely that would have been the honest thing to do? If honesty was to play any part.'

He gave an unmirthful smile. He was suffering from the revelation, but was not quite defeated. 'Ah! There you hit the difficult point – the place of indecision. It always comes, I suspect, in such matters. There is no simple, signposted way forward. I had you – and the children. There was – as you have just reminded me – the terrible time of Rebecca—'

'But all the while,' I said, as new distances were opening, 'you had this comfort, this other family. You had your son.'

Jasper was on his feet. I saw his height – Alexander's height. 'You must understand, Mrs St Clair, that for a long time *I* didn't know the truth. Perhaps of small importance ... but there it was.'

I turned to Alexander. 'You mean ... you didn't *tell* him? Your own son?'

'My dear Isabel, as I've just said, there are no plain paths. I had to take every care. I still do.'

He faced Jasper, as if he challenged him. But I thought Jasper met the challenge – he was not after all a boy any more, and whatever scars his unconventional upbringing had brought him he kept hidden. He said, 'Yes, sir, that is perfectly understood. You were an intermittent visitor –' I saw Alexander flinch '– but of course as I grew older, the situation became, let's say, of interest to me. I began to wonder... Particularly, as, you must admit, there's a likeness between us. So that when I learned the truth from my mother, it came as no great surprise.'

149

'Your mother,' Alexander said, 'has had a difficult life. Without the protection of a husband, or the promise of a future companion.'

'However,' Jasper said, 'she made you pay for that.'

I was for a moment discomfited. I saw the figure of Leonora Vye, dark, handsome, no longer young, separated now, it seemed, from Alexander, and spoken of with detachment, even disdain, by her son. I could in the circumstances have no love for her, but I had some pity.

Jasper went on, 'It's understandable, of course. As you say, Father, it has not been an easy life. But I have tried to persuade her that there's no need to trouble you further. I am a man now, with means enough to keep her at least from any hardship. But – ' he gave a wry smile '– a woman with a sense of wrong has much buried anger. She insists on pursuing her own course.'

'She wants,' Alexander said, 'her last drop of blood.'

'It seems so, sir. Yes, it seems so.'

'And now,' I said, 'there is something about Gilbert Duvane?'

'He's a danger,' Jasper said.

Alexander broke in, 'He's a fool! He wants to ruin me – and much good will it do him!'

'Revenge,' said Jasper, 'seldom does any good. But it's said to be sweet.'

Alexander shrugged. 'I shall continue to pay him the interest on his investments, mostly, as he understands it, Government Securities. But when it comes to producing a capital sum – that will need careful handling. But it can be done.'

'It can be done how?' I asked.

Alexander kept his eyes on his hands which turned slightly together. 'The position,' he said, 'isn't difficult to understand. I look after the capital investments of various parties – wills left in favour of diverse families, old ladies with no issue who want to divide their estates among distant members of their family. Or cats' homes. I pay the interest on these legacies, coming from such things as India Stock, Consuls. They pay three and a half to four per cent. Their recipients are never disappointed.'

Jasper was watching me with an expression of sympathetic

150

interest. I felt a constriction in my chest, as if I were faced with a dangerous step over a ravine. 'But the capital?' I said.

'That has been in my hands. At times I've had to – let's say – distribute it as I thought best. When it comes to a time, for instance, of a child's coming of age, it has been necessary to sell out in one case to produce the money in another. I have been careful. There have been times when I've sailed close to the wind. But I've kept afloat. In all this time I've never been...'

'Rumbled, sir?' Jasper said.

Alexander took no offence. 'If you like.'

'But,' I said, 'in all this time you were running the risk?'

'Oh, yes, Isabel dear; a great risk. But I have succeeded. And, God willing, shall continue to succeed. In spite of Gilbert Duvane. He thinks he's a clever young man and, like all clever young men, he likes the idea of bringing down a man older and more successful than himself. But I can outdo him. I have more experience of life and finance than he has.' He glanced from me to Jasper, then said with a trace of exasperation, 'You may not believe me, but I can.'

Jasper said, 'You've certainly succeeded so far, sir.' But his face was turned to me.

I said, 'I understand what you've been doing. So far you haven't been found out. But if you *were* found out?'

'I should go to prison.' He gave it without emphasis, a statement of fact.

I took this in. I said, 'Of course Beatrice has known all along?'

A brief glance from Alexander. 'I had to tell someone.'

'And she knew also about Leonora – and her son?'

'That goes without saying.'

I could remember Beatrice, denying any knowledge of Alexander's 'affair', that day on the island. Nothing was certain anymore.

Jasper rose to his feet. 'Perhaps, as the son concerned, it would be better for me to leave you now. Believe me, Mrs St Clair, I'd help you, if I could. Perhaps ... perhaps one day I shall be able to. Goodbye, Father. Goodbye, Mrs St Clair.'

As the door closed on him, I faced Alexander. The room was different now we were alone. I said, 'But whatever

151

happens, the threat remains? Something might go wrong – you might find yourself in court, with everything lost?'

He gave a shrug. 'That hasn't happened yet.'

'No, not yet. But—'

'I've told you the whole story. You must make of it what you will. It was never my intention that you should know anything.'

'I should imagine not.'

'What made you come? Here, this morning?'

I hesitated. To say that I had come because of an anonymous message would make him either scornful – or, perhaps, alarmed. I said, 'I've not been happy for some time. As I told you, I had a feeling that something was wrong.'

He looked at me as if he were trying to believe my words.

Then he said, 'It was most unfortunate timing.'

That did not need an answer. There in the room, spread out like a map, was the history of our marriage, of Alexander's double life, of his other son. It would take time, I thought, to come to terms with that long story of deception and intrigue. What was I to make of him? A buccaneer who believed he could bestride two loves, keep two families, casting doubt to the winds? Perhaps. But I could remember also the man who had shown tenderness to me, there on the island; who had grieved in his own way for the loss of his children.

I didn't want to dwell on this aspect of Alexander; it confused me. It would be simpler to feel only anger, even outrage. The jealousy at least of hurt pride. Perhaps in a sense I did feel these things, but they were in some way uncomfortably inhibited. I wanted chiefly to get away from Alexander and the confusion he was causing me. But I would have to stay the night in the London house. The next day I would go, I would return to the island.

I said as much to Alexander, and he looked up at me, his face drawn with heavy lines. I thought with Jasper's departure, panache had gone out of him. 'You wish to go? Yes, I suppose that's understandable.' He appeared to hesitate, then said, 'We shall have to discuss the future.'

I hadn't in truth thought about the future, beyond my need to return to the island the next day. But he went on, getting to his feet, becoming, I thought, more like the old Alexander, 'My hope is that the marriage will continue.'

The words seemed to me so formal, indeed, so extraordinary, that I felt they must refer to someone else.

'But we have no marriage!' I protested.

'You may think that now, Isabel. But it is not quite true.'

I hadn't thought that Alexander could surprise me anymore, but with this he had succeeded. I repeated, 'We have no marriage, Alexander. Perhaps we never had.'

He didn't answer me. The wild thought crossed my mind that I had perhaps wounded him? I waited a moment longer, in case he would find some word, but when he did not, I left the room, glad to go. Now I only wanted to be quit of the house which had even more the elements of a prison.

I returned next day to the island. I went with that sense of deep relief which comes with escape. I was getting away, leaving the London house, leaving Alexander. Leaving Leonora and Jasper Vye. These two figures had persisted through my night's dreams. Jasper puzzled me, for he seemed to cast some benign influence – yet he was Alexander's son by another woman. And he lived, while Toby... Yes, I was glad to go.

On the ferry I let the salt wind blow on my face. Let it all go, I thought; let the past slip away, like the wake of the ferry. Return again to the place I loved, never mind what sorrow I had known there.

Rosecroft again. The place where I belonged, where from the open window came the pulse of the sea. When I had changed from my travelling clothes and unpacked my case, I found the letter which had taken me to London. Its sting had been almost drawn – almost, not quite. For there was this person, unknown to me, yet closely aware of Alexander's private concerns. 'Such letters should be ignored,' Piers had said, but I had not ignored it and still could not entirely put it out of my mind.

I left the house and made my way by the path that led on to the Down. I didn't want to meet Piers yet; I had too much to tell him, and too much uncertainty in my own mind.

But one makes decisions, and life, of course, even in the smallest aspect, doesn't abide by them. As I took my way on to the higher level of the Down, I saw him coming towards me.

I stood still. I wanted to say, 'I am not ready,' but I was silent. He said, 'I heard you'd come back,' and I asked how this was possible, but he said that rumours ran fast in this small place.

I walked with him, and was for a moment greatly comforted by his presence beside me. Having been in the London room, in an atmosphere of revelation and deceit, the warm sensations of love and trust flowed through me. Yet I was still unready to face him with the full truth.

He asked me to come back to his house, but I said I wanted to stay in the open air. He gave me then a brief glance of amusement, as if to say that I had no need to fear being alone with him. I shook my head, smiling too, and said that I simply needed the open air and the sight of the sea, after the time in London.

We sat together, there on Tennyson Down. I drew in great breaths of salty air, as if I drew in release from that encounter in the London room. I glanced at Piers beside me, aware that I saw him with a difference. The love I felt was no less, but the new knowledge of Alexander changed the air between us. Not a change I was comfortable with.

Piers asked me what I had learned and there, on the familiar Down, with the sea below us, I told him the story. He nodded from time to time, showing no surprise. The unchanging expression on his face at first puzzled then irked me a little. 'You don't consider it strange?'

He gave his usual wry smile. 'I too have had a revelation. To begin with, I know who wrote you the letter.'

'You *know*?'

'She came yesterday. A young woman. You may perhaps remember her – know her. She looks a bit wild, rather beautiful, copper-coloured hair, served sometimes at the inn.'

I sat still. Oh yes, I knew her. Red hair blown in the wind, large eyes, greenish and distrustful. I had seen her wandering at the edge of the shore barefoot, her shoes in her hand, her skirt lifted. I even knew her name – Meg Sanderson. 'That girl? *She* wrote – but why?'

'She'd been to see me before. When I was rector, and later when I became – let's say – a kind of fellow traveller. She was one of those who need to talk at length, and with no great tendency to listen. But I was sorry for her. Not much of an inheritance – father drank and beat her mother – herself too, sometimes.'

'But me – why did she write to me?'

'It turns out – I've only just learned this, yesterday – that she was in love, or at any rate obsessed with, Jasper Vye.'

'With Jasper?'

'And he, I understand, with her. Apparently he confided in her – told her what he knew of his parentage – unguardedly, I admit, but men, when they're physically carried away, say unwise things.'

'But the letter?'

'Yes – that's what made her come to me. Jasper had, it seemed, found her too much for him. Which one can readily understand: she's a troubled and troubling young woman. He made it clear that he didn't want to see her any more. You can imagine how she'd respond to that.'

I saw Meg Sanderson, her pretty face marred with anger.

'But as soon as she'd delivered the letter, she regretted it. She came to me – and for the first time mentioned the name of Jasper Vye. She said that she felt it her duty to "make you aware of the position". But of course that wasn't the real reason. Her object was Jasper, and some way in which she could wound him.'

'But in the event,' I said, 'it wasn't Jasper who was wounded.'

Piers shrugged. 'Random fire – that was all she was capable of.'

'Could she be a danger?' I asked, and he made a small grimace. 'One can't know. She's an unpredictable young woman. And angry and unhappy. It's possible, of course, that Jasper, in spite of himself might be drawn back to her. As I say, one can't know.'

I said, 'She has no quarrel with Alexander?'

He glanced quickly at me as I mentioned the name, but said only, 'No ... but she knows perhaps more than she should.'

I had brought the letter with me and looked at the unknown hand, the large, scrawling letters. So Meg Sanderson, the local wild girl, had sent me to London, to confront Alexander.

Piers said, 'And now?'

I folded the letter. I didn't ask what lay behind his question. I said, 'I have two children...'

'Scarcely children any more.'

155

'They trouble me.'

'I imagine children will trouble parents to the end of time.'

'Even so...'

'What difference can it make to them if you leave Alexander? Dear God, look what he's done to you!'

I sat there, with the sea below us. I shivered, though the air was warm. I could see Alexander in the London room, head bowed, with the threat on him. I had every reason, as Piers said, to cut myself off from that image. And yet...

I said, trying to control my distress, 'So much has happened. My whole world turned upside down – or so it seems. I've still not got my breath back.'

Yes, he said; that he understood. (We had both, as if by comment consent, risen to our feet.) 'But, my dearest love, you have to make a decision.' We were standing close; his hands on my shoulders were trembling, and I was afraid. 'You *have* to make a decision,' he repeated. 'There will never be a good time, there will never be an easy time. My poor darling, you must know that. It can't be done without effort and some pain. But if we're not to throw away the chance of happiness – or if that's too easy a word, some fulfilment – then we have to do it. Take the difficult step. Or *you* do. I've already made up my mind.'

'I know – I know.' I tried to hold back the tears, for he was growing angry, and I couldn't bear his anger. I said I had responsibilities that he was free from, but he wouldn't listen.

'There's a whole life, Isabel. Or what is left of a life – we are neither of us young. Nothing will wait for us. We shall be old, with this love just thrown away. That is a waste, when so much of life is waste.'

Yes, I thought, I knew about waste. The waste of life, of Toby's, of Rebecca's. The years lost. And my own years, those to come. To be spent with Piers, whom I loved, whom I longed for? The decision loomed large ahead of me, too great for me at this moment. I muttered, 'Alexander—'

Piers almost shouted, 'You owe *nothing* to Alexander! Nothing at all! No – don't turn away. My darling, please don't turn away. It's possible to lose everything!' He spoke with a kind of anguish, and I wanted to shut my ears to it. I couldn't leave him, yet I wanted to escape, for the moment was too much for me.

He grasped my hand, but I pulled it from him, and made my way down the path, towards the house. He called my name once, as I went, but he did not follow me.

That night I lay awake for a long time. Morning didn't bring me the ease of decision. But I was becoming certain of one thing – I couldn't finally part from Piers. I had found a love that seemed larger than the sorrows I had known, larger than fear. I wanted to say, 'Oh, please wait for me; give me time.' After breakfast I walked a little way, to that point where I could see the poet's house. The poet whose words had so greatly comforted me. They seemed to echo on the air, snatches of the verse that had so entranced me, again offering comfort...

> Behold, we know not anything;
> I can but trust that good shall fall
> At last – far off – at last, to all,
> And every winter change to spring.

How did it go on?

> So runs my dream: but what am I?
> An infant crying in the night:
> An infant crying for the light:
> And with no language but a cry.

Almost, I thought, I could see the old man, walking there, above the sea.

Chapter 16
Kate and Perdita – 1940

The day darkened early. As Kate drew the black-out curtains the sirens sounded, the familiar plangent wail.

'Oh, damn!' Perdita said: 'Will he come?' for the name of Jasper Vye had threaded the day. Kate said yes, he'd come; he hadn't sounded like a man who'd be bothered by air raids.

'What *did* he sound like?' Perdita spoke with abiding curiosity and Kate said he sounded unruffled and friendly, and not likely to be late – or no later than need be, in the Blitz.

Indeed, he arrived almost on time. His face, Kate thought, was familiar from the funeral, his manner at ease, informal, as if this encounter were nothing extraordinary. She looked at him with absorbed interest, for he was not only the man in his sixties with the lines scored on his face, but the young man who had stood in the London room, and whose mother had overturned Isabel's life; who had as a boy run on the island shore.

Intermittent anti-aircraft fire formed a background to the encounter. Jasper, Kate observed, paid no attention to the sound. He met their interest (Kate and Perdita's) with a lively interest of his own: his dark eyes beneath heavy eyebrows gleamed with a kind of triumph. 'So I'm here at last!' he seemed to say though he didn't put it into words.

When they were sitting at the supper table, the ordinary civilities done, Kate said, 'Why've you waited till now to get in touch with us? You don't live far away, and you knew about us, you knew where I lived.'

He brooded, looking at the level of wine in his glass. 'I think perhaps, as long as your grandmother, Isabel, was alive I felt – let's say – debarred from you. I came from the wrong side of the blanket.'

'Did that matter?' Perdita asked, and he said after further thought, yes, he thought perhaps it did. All things considered, he added.

'We knew nothing of you – not till we read those.' She pointed to the pile of journals and gave him some of the details of the many pages.

'So she wrote it all down!' Jasper exclaimed. 'That I never knew.'

'She wrote it down,' Kate said, 'until a meeting with Piers Malleson, after her return from London, when she confronted you and your mother. And there it stops. Or perhaps she wrote more, but it's not survived.'

Jasper poured wine from the bottle which he had brought to accompany the meal of cheese and dried-egg omelette and sand-coloured bread. He said, 'Something survived.'

'More books?' Perdita asked with excitement, but he shook his head. 'I'll tell you. All in good time. First of all, there was Alexander. He felt more and more the strain of his business, the threat from Gilbert Duvane. However, by one of those happy turns of fate there was someone ready to step in and – shall we say – save the bacon.'

One eyebrow twitched, as Kate with Perdita beside her looked at him with spellbound curiosity. Then Kate said, with a flash of understanding, '*You*. That's why there was no outright scandal, no prosecution ... *you* took it on.'

Jasper looked ironically mischievous, pleased, but not over-whelmingly so, Kate thought. 'Well ... I was qualified when Alexander ran into trouble. When Gilbert Duvane put the heat on. I knew the whole story. I knew it from both sides, as it were. So what could be better? Except of course for Isabel. For I was not her son, and she found it hard to accept that I had taken over the chaos that Alexander left.' A louder burst of gunfire made him turn his head. 'How small it seems, that old duplicity. And yet at the time ... it loomed large.'

Perdita looked at him, wide-eyed. 'You mean you set the business to rights? All of it?'

Again the lift of an eyebrow. 'It took time. And trouble, of course. But we all have certain gifts – I believe St Paul says so

159

somewhere. I have a gift for dealing with complex finance. Not a very noble one, perhaps, but useful on occasion. In a way, I even enjoy it as some men I believe enjoy driving through difficult traffic. I was fortunate, perhaps. Lucky at cards, they say, don't they, unlucky in love? Put money in place of cards, that's how it's been for me.'

Not sorry for himself, Kate thought, but sad about it.

She said, 'There was Meg Sanderson...'

'Ah!' His brows lifted again and his eyes sparked. 'Yes, indeed, there was Meg. You've read about her? She was a wild one, and very beautiful. "I met a lady in the meads..." That sort of thing. In the end, against my better judgment, I married her.'

'Married!' Kate exclaimed, and Jasper smiled. 'Oh yes ... people's lives are endlessly surprising. But ... it didn't work. One wouldn't have expected it to. It was, however, one way of keeping her silent, wasn't it? She knew a great deal.'

'Isabel was afraid of what she might say, what she might do,' Kate put in, and Jasper nodded.

'All the same – she wasn't a malicious girl. Quick to anger, but not deliberately cruel. However, she fell out of love with me. Grew bored, and went off with another man, an artist – quite well known in later years. He painted her picture and it found its way into the Tate Gallery. I didn't marry again – I decided it was not my metier.' He drank from his glass. 'So I can only count my success in life in financial terms. Rather a dry harvest.'

'Seems to me,' Kate said, 'you've done some valuable work.'

'Mmm ... well. I'd like, if possible, to do more. I have an idea that may appeal to you. We'll come to it in due course. Well!' he exclaimed as the room trembled with the fall of high explosive, 'that was close – d'you want to go to a shelter?'

Kate shook her head, and Perdita said, 'Gosh, no. I want to hear more. How you managed grandfather's mess. How you got it straight.'

Jasper looked at her, Kate thought, with affectionate amusement. 'Details would be tedious now. I can't deny that there were difficult times. Times when I wondered if I was not going to be shown up – or even shut up. But it seemed to me that as my mother had been at the root of Alexander's original fraud, it was apt that I should do my best to restore the status quo. I had a certain satisfaction in achieving that.'

'And Isabel...?' Kate began.

'She was grateful. But I was Alexander's son ... it wasn't easy for her. So I never became part of the family, as you might say.'

'Pity,' Perdita said. 'As a family, we need friends.'

Jasper smiled. 'Oh, I was very curious about you all. About Marigold and Sylvia – and their children: the two of you. I watched you from the wings.'

'Nice thought,' Kate said. 'But when Grandmother died?'

'Yes, then I felt free to make myself known to you. It seemed, as I say, that Isabel had given me her blessing. That may seem strange to you, for I'm not a sentimental man. I have few dreams, and those I have I rarely expect to be fulfilled.'

Kate met his glance then; it almost seemed as if he asked her a question. He had a kind of magic, she reflected, because he had stepped from the faded pages of Isabel's diary into this wartime room. 'But surely,' she said, 'we should have known *some*thing about you? Until we read the journals we didn't even know your name.'

'No ... but you have to remember that the world cracked apart in 1914, after Toby's death. Perhaps that death was only a little premature – perhaps he would have gone with so many other young men. The kaleidoscope changes as one looks back.'

'And you?' Kate said, while an ambulance siren tore the air apart outside.

'I was – in that First War – an elderly Staff Officer. All of us, I suppose, who saw something of that war were changed. The world felt lonely afterwards. I left the St Clair finances in good shape. For a time I went abroad, to live in France. The place was after all familiar. I went into the aircraft business. It was a good move. No one much believed in it then – or only a few. But that, as I've told you, was my metier – knowing where the money would be.'

This, Kate thought, is leading up to something – but I'm not yet sure what it is. 'You did well?' she asked.

He said, 'Very well. I returned to this country from time to time. I made discreet enquiries about the St Clairs – the business was long out of my hands, the time of threat passed. And Isabel had two grandchildren.' He looked from one to the other of them with a dry smile of recognition. 'Their births lifted her heart. A friend who gave me news of her said that she seemed to throw off sadness.'

'A friend?' Perdita asked, chin on her hands.

'Ah. Well, yes; that I suppose is the essence of the story.' He made a small gesture to the pile of journals. 'Piers Malleson. Isabel's great love.'

Kate again met his glance, as if a question remained. 'What happened?' she asked. 'I've often thought – "These lovers fled away into the storm" – but they couldn't have. Isabel was a widow when Grandfather died, and she didn't marry again.'

'No. She didn't leave Alexander. Though pretty frail, he lived a long life. But ...' He took a letter from his wallet. 'There was a time – I suppose you'd say, of borrowed happiness. I think that describes it.' As he unfolded the letter, he went on, 'Alexander in his "decline" – stayed in London. From time to time, Isabel escaped to the island. And there –' he shrugged '– well, she and Piers spent time together. Threatened time – but all time is, isn't it? They were close together in the place she loved – on that shore, where the children played – where indeed I played myself.' The letter was spread before him. He said, 'This came to me from Piers, after his death. I think, now that they're both gone, you should see it. Isabel's letter.'

He pushed the faded piece of paper towards them. Together, Kate and Perdita bent their heads over it. The familiar writing, Kate thought, aware of Perdita close beside her. She read:

'My dearest love,
   Now that I am returned to London, and you are to leave the island, I write this in much gratitude. I have known a happiness which seems to be more than I deserved. I have loved you with a love which somehow enfolded the love I had for my children – for Toby and Rebecca. Enfolded everything. Does this make sense? Perhaps not, but I think you'll understand. You said to me once (quoting, I think), "Those who love beyond the world cannot be separated by it". Whatever happens now, I do not believe I can be

162

separated from you. So I shall not say "Goodbye" – just that my love goes on. Isabel.'

Jasper said, taking the letter, 'That was when she returned to London to care for Alexander who was going downhill. But Rosecroft remained her property – I saw to that.'

Kate saw the house which had been a haven for Charles and herself. '"Those who love beyond the world,"' she said, 'I like that.' For the moment she was aware of Isabel, walking beside her lover... What were the words in the journal? Something about 'that other girl in a difficult love in a different time'. She said, 'And Piers?'

'He left the island. We had become friends, at first through Meg. He left the Church too, but he lived out its teaching, at least, as I understand it. He spent his time caring for the poor – when war came, being too old for active service, he drove an ambulance, and cared for the sick. Afterwards he worked with the disabled and the shell-shocked – of which, as you know, there were many. We met from time to time – he never married, so that when Meg had gone, we were both without family, both strangers as it were to the world of children and grandchildren. But he was making some good of his life, and I – well, I was able to give to the charities he worked for. It's always possible for men like myself to salve their consciences by giving money which they can afford to give.'

He looked from one to the other, Kate thought, with a smile that had a question in it: as if he had something to say which gave him pause ... something of importance? Yes, Kate thought, I think so. He doesn't – he can't possibly – know that I'm pregnant with Charles' child. But there's a change in the room, as if a hand were held out to me... The clang of a rescue lorry sounded from the street. A man's voice echoed, giving orders.

Jasper pushed an empty plate to one side. He smiled at them, as if with faint apology. 'I do have a real reason for wanting to see you – apart from curiosity, that is. As I've told you, I've done well financially. I have no wife or children. My mother has gone, some years ago now. I'm content enough with my state – I'm not one to spend much time repining. But it leaves me with a difficulty.'

163

He looked at them with that familiar dry amusement, as if the difficulty gave him some embarrassment. He said, 'I have bequeathed my assets mainly to Isabel's family – that is, to you, Kate and Perdita. No! Please don't say anything. There's no acceptable way of responding to an announcement of future legacies. Perhaps one day someone will find one, but so far as I know they haven't yet. As I say, you are my beneficiaries. But I'm not quite satisfied with that.'

Kate said, 'How – not satisfied? To say the least it sounds generous.'

'Generosity doesn't really come into it. My will can't do any good until after my death – which in these circumstances may be the next ten minutes or perhaps another twenty years – men survive wars and live to be old.' Again he looked from one to the other. 'So I hope you'll give me permission – and the pleasure – of accepting a sum of money for each of you which I will prepare with my solicitor to invest... No! I've told you, I don't want thanks. Just acceptance.'

'How can we possibly—' Perdita began.

Jasper interrupted. 'Easily, I should hope. Some might say I have rather an empty life. Time moves on. Soon – not so long ahead – I shall be an old man. To know that I'd made life a little easier for two of Isabel's descendants would be gratifying. Perhaps even a man who's decided to live alone has some vestigial dreams of a family. I shouldn't make any demands on you – you can't buy your way into people's lives. When it's possible again – I shall travel. I should be a casual visitor. Only different from others because we both remember Isabel, who was your grandmother. And that Alexander was my father. So that I am, you might say, a flawed uncle?'

The raid had drawn closer; the guns slammed at the sky. The room shivered a little, as if with shock. Kate looked at this strange munificence: the old Kate who would have automatically said no to any unsolicited offer of cash was for the moment overcome by the prospect which now, it seemed, lay before her.

'You both need time, of course,' Jasper said, as they cleared the table. 'I understand that. But the offer isn't made out of patronage – its something which has been in my mind for some while.' On waking, he said, when the faint heaviness of the day

164

oppressed him, as it sometimes did, the idea had lifted his spirits. 'And I'm sure,' he added, 'you'd both like to do that.'

Persuaded by Kate, he stayed until the guns quietened. Near midnight the all clear sounded, the single note flying out like a banner over the city. Standing in the hall, preparing to go, Jasper said he had one last request.

'Golly, anything,' Perdita said, and he smiled.

'Her ashes are, I understand, to be scattered on the island. Somewhere above the bay. And I'd like to be there... Is that too much to ask?' he said, with a rare hint of diffidence, and was passionately reassured.

'Good. Good. One will have to get permission, of course – those other islands, Guernsey and Jersey, are occupied by the enemy. But that can be arranged.'

He said goodbye, with a small look of triumph, as if some game had been won. When he'd gone, Kate turned out the light, opened the black-out curtains and watched him as he walked, dimly visible in the moonlit dark, going with that loneliness which all solitary figures show when they're observed, unaware.

Perdita asked if it had really happened? And could they possibly accept his offer? Was it *true*?

But Kate was past questions; she was lost in this interweaving of two worlds, the sensation of a door opening on an unlooked-for hope.

Chapter 17

Kate and Perdita – 1940
The Island

The day was cold, there were even small flurries of snow. Kate paused to take in this first sight of the wartime island, the familiar places scored with outlines of defence: barbed wire, metal scaffolding and concrete drums on the beaches. Shrimping nets and beach balls, the barefoot, brown-legged children, shouting over the wash of the sea were gone; the island was full of troops, uniforms everywhere. A small flame of inspiration touched her: sometime, she thought, maybe I could write about this – the two islands.

Jasper walked through the confusion of this wartime outpost with a kind of courteous assurance. He had arranged rooms at the hotel once known as Plumbley's; the hotel was full of soldiers, but he had, surprisingly but aptly, secured rooms for Kate, Perdita and himself. He had the small casket of ashes.

The window of Kate's room gave on to a balcony from which she could see the stretch of shore with its strange-shaped rock: the rock like a table for sacrifice, Beatrice had said. But now the coils of barbed wire sprouted like ungainly plants, thorn-edged, and the sea drove with winter strength over the concrete drums. But there was no enemy yet – except from the air. Clouds of Heinkels and Messerschmitts, it was said, swarmed over the island, heading for the cities beyond. And from the bombed cities strong winds picked up the charred litter of war and carried it to the island.

Perdita joined Kate on the balcony. She was companionable, not saying much. Together they looked out towards the far coast, enemy-occupied; its nearness gave menace to the sea.

Kate glanced at Perdita, aware of the danger to Gerald as he crossed that enemy coast.

They went out, with Jasper, into the cold, armoured island. They wore scarves, heavy jackets, gloves, woollen or fur hats. The wind pummelled them like a rough schoolboy and the sea exploded on the shore. Notices everywhere warned 'WD. KEEP OUT', but they were able to find a pathway up on to the Down. The wind was stronger there, their eyes watered and they hadn't much breath for speech.

Jasper led them a little way down to a coign where the wind was less. (He did, after all, Kate reflected, know the island of old; he played there as a boy. The boy whom Isabel had sought for at the sea's edge.) Within the coign gorse showed a few yellow flowers; the roughened sea drove the spray high, almost to cliff top. Here there was a little shroud of silence, as if wind and sea were on the other side of thickened glass.

Jasper gave Kate the casket. She felt at once awkward and apprehensive, like all those who say farewell, whether at railway station or burial ground. Above the shore where Isabel's children had played, she let the ash drift on the wintry air. Perdita was beside her, solemn, hands deep in her pockets; Jasper stood, hunched in heavy overcoat, masculine, face carved in heavy lines. He said, 'She is gone now.'

But Kate was powerfully aware of her. Down there on the shore, more real than the defences of wire and concrete, were the figures of Marigold, Rebecca, Sylvia and Toby. Children, not old, not subject to time.

Children. She faced the secret she had shared with Perdita – the prospect which she had thought, if it was true, to cancel, brutally to forgo. But now she knew a sensation of warmth where before there had been only pain. Charles' son or daughter. She could offer this to Isabel; it seemed to give an answer. For a moment she could see the shore restored to sunlight and the shrill voices. And a child running there. Jasper's prodigality would help to make it possible.

She looked at him as he stood there in the sheltering hollow. He was a benign presence, still magically bestriding past and present. But he would, of course, soon be on to other things; they had to leave the island and he would be lost in the crowded wartime life to which they were all subject now. And

167

Perdita would return to her children in Cumberland, where she must wait for news of Gerald, bound nightly for that enemy coast. There is no certainty, Kate thought; we are all parting, all the time.

They turned to climb the path together, their task done. She is gone now, Jasper had said. Yes, gone; you could make nothing of dispersed ash – there was no person anymore to talk or weep. And yet the words Kate had read in the journals still haunted her – 'that other girl in a difficult love in a different and future time...'

They went back to the hotel, where the many soldiers and their equipment, the world of war and immediate danger surrounded but did not quite encompass them. They sat together in the crowded bar, warmed by a rare ration of spirits. Talk surged about them, mostly about dogfights overhead, or plane crashes on the island. A man spoke of the night when a stream of bombers had droned overhead for eleven hours – the night of the Coventry raid, he said...

For a second Kate looked aside. It was like stretching out an arm and almost touching Charles' hand. She would have liked to give him reassurance: reassurance about his child.

Jasper talked of future plans. He was confident, at home in this occupied place, as he seemed to be at home anywhere. His presence, Kate thought, had stamped itself upon this whole undertaking with a kind of love and assurance.

It was time to go.

They grouped together with their hand luggage, Perdita wrapping a scarf about her. Kate could still hear the sea. They exchanged easy words, as if this were the end of some ordinary visit. Kate glanced back once, to see the shape of the cliffs and the shore, as Isabel must have seen them.

She would tell Perdita about her decision; not yet. Jasper too, perhaps.

They were on their way, leaving the island behind. A soldier asked for their passes; the sky darkened and there was again a flurry of snow.

Now for the ferry.